"You're out of line, Mitchell Waring."

His eyes followed her jerky progress as she backed away from him warily. "Perhaps." Then he canceled his agreement. "But only at the beginning. You want me, Brandy."

It was true! Every word he'd uttered was true. Resentment of him, of her newly discovered weakness, put iron into her resolve and steel into her voice.

"All I want is for you to get out of here."

A small, unnervingly understanding smile lifted the corners of his tight-lipped mouth.

"All right. I won't push it," he promised. "At least not tonight. But listen carefully. Your days of freedom are numbered—my love."

Mitch's smile spread at her gasp of protest at the endearment. Then he was gone, his quiet laughter drifting back from the stairway to torment her.

WELCOME
TO THE WONDERFUL WORLD
OF *Harlequin Romances*

Interesting, informative and entertaining,
each Harlequin Romance portrays an appealing
and original love story. With a varied array
of settings, we may lure you on an African safari,
to a quaint Welsh village, or an exotic Riviera
location—anywhere and everywhere that adventurous
men and women fall in love.

As publishers of Harlequin Romances, we're
extremely proud of our books. Since 1949,
Harlequin Enterprises has built its publishing
reputation on the solid base of quality and
originality. Our stories are the most popular
paperback romances sold in North America; every
month, six new titles are released and sold at
nearly every book-selling store in Canada and the
United States.

For a list of all titles currently available,
send your name and address to:

HARLEQUIN READER SERVICE,
(In the U.S.) P.O. Box 52040, Phoenix, AZ 85072-2040
(In Canada) P.O. Box 2800, Postal Station A
5170 Yonge Street, Willowdale, Ont. M2N 5T5

We sincerely hope you enjoy reading
this Harlequin Romance.

Yours truly,

THE PUBLISHERS
Harlequin Romances

Candleglow

Amii Lorin

Harlequin Books

TORONTO • NEW YORK • LONDON
AMSTERDAM • PARIS • SYDNEY • HAMBURG
STOCKHOLM • ATHENS • TOKYO • MILAN

Original hardcover edition published in 1983
by Mills & Boon Limited

ISBN 0-373-02662-5

Harlequin Romance first edition December 1984

For
NORM WENGER
candlemaker, craftsman, valued friend

CHAPTER ONE

'BRAND, where's my shirt?'

Brandy grimaced at the shrill sound of her sister's voice before calling patiently, 'What shirt, Bev?'

'You know,' the fourteen-year-old shouted. 'The one with the "Boss" on the back.' An overdrawn groan drifted from the second floor to the kitchen, where Brandy was gingerly turning bacon in a black frying pan. 'If Karen wore that shirt today I'll jump up and down on her dumb head!'

The boss? Brandy frowned. Oh, the Springsteen shirt, the one Bev had happily plunked down the majority of her spending money for at that stand on the boardwalk last summer.

Now Brandy groaned. Bev loved that shirt. If Karen had filched it this morning there would be war in the house this evening!

The sizzling bacon aimed and spat, striking Brandy on the back of her hand.

'Oh, damn!'

Flicking on the cold water tap, Brandy thrust her hand into the gush of water. She had seen that shirt; but where? Patting her hand dry, she frowned in concentration, visualising her sister's favourite garment. Black, with a likeness of the rock star on the front and, yes, a pair of sneakers and a guitar on the back.

A light clicked on in her mind and the frown was replaced with a smile. Using tongs, she transferred the bacon from the pan to a paper-towel-covered plate.

After turning off the burner, she walked to the foot of the back stairs.

'Bev,' Brandy called, but not loudly enough to penetrate her young sister's grumbling of mayhem if, indeed, her year older sibling had had the temerity to wear *her* shirt that morning.

'Bev!' Brandy had to shout. 'Will you stop grousing and answer me?'

'Well?' The small form of Brandy's sister appeared at the top of the stairs, her gamine face set in mutinous lines.

'I think I may have put your shirt in my sweater drawer by mistake. Go and look before you blow a fuse.' Brandy smiled as the small figure, seemingly electrified, spun away. 'Then come down for breakfast,' she called after the teenager.

Five minutes later, wearing her beloved shirt, Bev strolled into the kitchen just as Brandy was sliding two sunny-side-up eggs on to a plate that now held two of the strips of crisp bacon.

'Man, I'm starving!' Bev declared dramatically.

'Man?' Brandy frowned. Turning from the stove, she was just in time to catch Bev in the act of inhaling her orange juice. 'Beverly!' she admonished. 'How many times have I told you not to gulp your juice?'

'I give up,' Bev chirped. 'How many times did you tell me?' The grin that revealed her small white teeth held pure devilry.

'I lost count long ago.' Brandy smiled gently at her pixie of a sister. Like everyone else who came into her sphere, Brandy could not withstand Bev's devil grin. 'I've also lost count of the number of times I've told you not to bolt your food, but I'll repeat it one more time, if I must.' She shook her head in despair at the rate of speed Bev was eating.

'Sorry,' Bev mumbled around a mouthful of bacon. 'I have to skip in five minutes. I have to meet Kim early so we can accidentally bump into Jack Denton as he leaves his house.'

'Accidentally?' Brandy arched her brows teasingly.

'Sure,' Bev flashed her heart-warming smile. 'We don't want him to know we're stalking him.' Wiping her lips with a paper napkin, she pushed away from the table.

During the following ninety seconds Brandy calmly sipped her coffee as the small live-wire tore around the house collecting her jacket, books and plastic gym bag. At the kitchen door she came to a momentary halt. 'I don't know what time I'll be home,' she informed her sister breathlessly. 'Rehearsals begin today.'

'I wasn't likely to forget,' Brandy drawled. 'It's been your main topic of conversation for weeks now. Good luck, honey.'

Another brief flash of her grin and Bev was gone, the door slamming behind her.

Wincing as the door made contact with the frame, Brandy refilled her cup with hot coffee and sat munching on the remaining piece of bacon as she contemplated the day ahead of her.

As it was Monday her shop was closed, but that in no way left her with idle time on her hands. The clothes hamper in the bathroom was on the point of overflowing with dirty laundry. Both the bathroom and the kitchen floors needed scrubbing. The fridge could use a thorough cleaning out. Added to the household chores, Brandy had her shop to dust and vacuum and the shelves to re-stock.

Grimacing at the offending floor beneath her feet, she set about clearing the table. Switching on the radio, she tuned in on an FM station that played music that did not attack the ears and, humming along, launched her own attack on the kitchen.

It was late afternoon before Brandy carried the upright vacuum cleaner into her shop as, par for Monday, one domestic job had led naturally into another.

Before starting the bathroom floor, she'd decided the medicine cabinet needed rearranging. While sorting the laundry, she found several garments that needed mending. Then, while putting the freshly laundered, neatly folded clothes away, she discovered numerous dresser drawers in dire need of straightening.

Now, her living quarters in reasonable order, a meat loaf mixed and baking alongside a family-sized box of frozen candied sweet potatoes, Brandy smiled as she surveyed her pride and joy; her shop, Candleglow.

The actual shop area was small, taking up what had once been the living room in the narrow three-storey row house. What had been the dining room was now a workroom, where Brandy moulded and carved her handcrafted candles. The kitchen was the only area on the ground floor used by the family.

The two upper stories of the old house comprised the family's living quarters. What had been the master bedroom was now used as a living room. The rest of the second floor contained two bedrooms and a rather old-fashioned bathroom. The smaller, third level was made up of two bedrooms and a storage room, that was in reality not much larger than a walk-in closet. The low-ceilinged basement was used exclusively for Brandy's shop supplies.

Brandy had taken a gamble on the shop. After discussing its feasibility with her father's attorney, she had invested nearly every dollar she possessed in converting the first floor of the house. Her gamble had paid off—if in a marginal way. She was free of debt, and until now, had been making a profit; albeit a small one.

The house being located on the fringes of Lancaster's shopping district had been the deciding factor—that and the fact that there was no other shop in the area dealing exclusively in candles. Brandy had banked heavily, and prayed fervently on the original, handmade product luring not only the shopping public but members of the business community as well. To a reasonable extent her prayers had been answered. She was approaching the fifth anniversary of her grand opening and, although she certainly wasn't swimming in money, thus far she had managed to stay afloat.

On entering the shop, Brandy deposited the vacuum cleaner to one side of the room, out of the way, and went directly to the small display window at the front of the building. Her critical gaze rested first on the candles arranged on its deeply recessed sill.

Come next Monday, she told herself, the window definitely had to be cleaned, and the display completely changed. That decision made, Brandy turned back to the room's interior and began her weekly job of dusting and re-stocking the shelves that lined both side walls and the long display counter that ran through the centre of the small room.

Her dusting and vacuuming were finished and she was fussing over the placement of various candles on the central counter when she heard the back door open and then close an instant before her sister Karen called:

'I'm home, Brand. Is there anything I can help you with?'

'Not in here,' Brandy called back. 'But you can check on the progress of the meat loaf in the oven, and then set the table for supper.'

'Will do,' Karen shouted over the sudden blare of rock music from the kitchen radio she had obviously just switched on.

'And turn that thing down, please,' Brandy shouted back, smiling at the oft-repeated order. All three of her sisters harboured a passion for rock—preferably loud.

Still smiling, Brandy stooped to select another candle from the storage shelves beneath the counter and was startled by the short, impatient-sounding trill of the front door bell. As she rose, her smile changed to a frown as another imperative blast of sound reverberated through the room.

'Okay, okay, hold your horses,' she muttered, brushing her hands over the faded jeans that clung lovingly to her hips. Despairing of all prospective customers who, apparently, could not read or comprehend the store hours stated clearly on the sign affixed to the outside of the solid, red-painted door, she crossed the room, sighing in exasperation at yet another resounding ring. Turning the lock, she swung the door open, fully prepared to educate the impatient shopper, but before the door was half way open, a harsh male voice attacked her ears.

'Does this young ... delinquent belong here?' the harshly arrogant voice demanded as a broad male hand indicated the cowering figure of Brandy's sister Darcy.

Anger, fierce and hot, surged through Brandy's entire being. Young delinquent? Darcy? *Her* sister? How dared he? Who is this clown? she wondered furiously. More to the point, who does he *think* he is? Her usually soft grey eyes glaring with hard defiance, Brandy ran a swift glance over the offensive-sounding male on her doorstep and felt an unwilling catch in her throat at the impressive look of him. Good lord, the man was a veritable tree!

From Brandy's very average height of five feet five and one half inches, the man seemed to tower over her like an oak. He had to be, at the very least, six feet three inches tall and, at that moment, every inch of him appeared taut with barely controlled fury. From her line of vision his shoulders seemed enormous, his flatly muscled chest a solid, imposing wall.

Glancing up at his face, Brandy felt the catch in her throat grow into a hard, painful lump. If his size called forth the picture of a tree, his roughly hewn features brought an image of chiselled granite.

This man was decidedly *not* handsome. All the bones in his face were too prominent, the planes too angular. His nose was too hawkish, his jaw too thrusting. Even the dark hair that covered his well shaped head was too much, the waves too crisp-looking, their healthy vibrancy too electrically charged with life. To crown the whole, he had the most riveting hazel eyes Brandy had ever encountered.

'Are you incapable of speech?' his harsh voice demanded. 'Or are you as dizzy as this young thief?'

'Thief?' His indictment dissolved the lump in her throat, releasing her vocal chords to vent her rage. 'Thief? Watch your mouth, buster. You're speaking about *my* sister!'

'Oh, Brandy, I'm sorry!'

The wail came from the trembling seventeen-year-old as she flung herself into Brandy's arms.

'Sorry for what, honey?' Brandy asked in confusion. Suddenly fresh anger was added to her confusion as the man moved forward, backing her, Darcy still clasped in her arms, clumsily into the shop.

'Who do you think you are?' Brandy gasped in time with the bang of the closing door.

'I don't *think*, I *know* who I am.' His hard-eyed gaze raked her dismissively. 'I *am* Mitchell Waring,' he informed her arrogantly. 'I *was* your sister's employer.'

'Was?' Brandy picked up on the emphasized past tense. 'What do you mean, was?'

'I mean exactly what I say—always,' Mitchell Waring bit out warningly. 'I don't keep on employees caught stealing from me.'

'Stealing?' Brandy repeated in a hoarse whisper, her arms tightening spasmodically around her now sobbing sister. 'But . . .'

'I have neither the time nor the inclination to go through this interview twice,' he cut her off sharply. 'If you'll go and summon either one or both of your parents, I'll . . .'

'Our parents are dead,' Brandy interrupted agitatedly. 'I'm Darcy's guardian . . .' her voice faltered momentarily at the derisive expression that crossed his face, then renewed anger sharpened her tone. 'You will explain your outrageous charge to *me*.'

'*You* are her guardian?' Mitchell Waring repeated with insulting incredulity. His eyes narrowed as he slowly raked his gaze over her from head to foot and back again.

Brandy's back stiffened in defence against the sensation of dismay that washed over her. She *knew* how unprepossessing she appeared at that moment.

Her old, faded jeans were a mite too tight over her rounded hips. Her baggy sweatshirt dated back to her college days, and gave evidence of every year of its existence. The moccasins that covered her stockingless feet were near the stage of total collapse. A soundless groan vibrated her vocal chords as an image of her untidy, unruly short curls, and her make-up-free, probably dust-coated face flashed through her mind. A disparaging twist to his lips left little doubt that his visual perusal exactly matched her mental image.

'That probably accounts for her behaviour.'

Brandy gulped back a gasp at this coldly uttered statement. Within the brief seconds required to make that all-encompassing survey, he had, very obviously, sized and measured her, and reached the conclusion that she was a cerebral featherweight.

Naturally incensed, yet strangely, vaguely hurt as well, Brandy opened her mouth to protest, only to be forestalled by a questioning voice from her workshop.

'What's the matter, Brand? Why is Darcy crying?'

Brandy had not even heard Bev—the youngest of the four sisters—enter the house. Bev's presence brought awareness of the rapidly waning afternoon.

'Did you say Darcy's crying?' Karen, following Bev into the workshop, made the family complete. With a half sob, half groan, Darcy hid her face in the curve of Brandy's shoulder.

'It's all right, girls,' Brandy strove for a reassuring tone. 'There's been a misunderstanding . . .'

'If there has been,' Mitchell Waring inserted angrily, 'it's on your part.' His sigh revealed growing impatience. 'Now, if there's somewhere we can discuss this in private?' He sliced a glance at the slim gold watch that circled his lightly haired, strong-looking wrist. 'I *do* have other things to do.'

Brandy had to fight down the urge to snap to attention at the note of command that laced his tone. Annoyed with herself for having the urge, she injected ice into her normally warm, somewhat husky voice.

'I'm sure you do.' Her soft grey eyes challenged his

hard hazel stare for a long moment before she very coolly turned her head to address her sisters. 'Why don't you two go finish supper while I straighten this mess out?'

Without waiting for a reply, she turned to the open stairway that rose to the second floor along the wall some five feet from the door. 'If you'll follow me, Mr Waring?' Disentangling Darcy, she clasped the trembling girl's hand and walked up the stairs that led to a hall running the length of the second floor.

After very politely ushering him into the living room and offering him a chair, which he declined, Brandy faced him like an enraged lioness whose young has been threatened.

'Now, what is this all about?' Drawn up to her full height, hands on her hips, grey eyes stormy with anger, indignant colour tinging her soft-skinned cheeks, Brandy had no idea how very appealing she looked to the tall man before her.

'Your sister was caught in the act of shoplifting this afternoon.' Mitchell Waring's cool hazel eyes calmly observed the effect of his blunt statement on Brandy's flushed face. Shock and disbelief fired her anger, lending beauty to her more then pretty face.

'You'd better be prepared to prove that charge.' Brandy hated the hoarse sound of her voice, yet there was something about the very steadiness of this man's gaze that tested her faith in her sister's honesty.

'I'm not stupid, Miss Styer.' A frown cut a groove between his eyes. 'Excuse me—*are* you Miss Styer, or are you married?'

'Miss Styer is correct.'

'Very well,' he clipped, the frown disappearing. 'As I was saying, I'm not stupid. I don't enjoy being informed of an employee—a well paid employee—

stealing from me. Nor do I make the mistake of levelling false accusations.' His gaze bored into hers unremittingly. 'Your sister is guilty, Miss Styer.'

All the anger and a great deal of confidence drained out of Brandy. Disappointment welled to fill the hollow she felt yawning inside. Unable to endure Mitchell Waring's unwavering stare, she lowered her lids.

'Perhaps you'd better sit down, Miss Styer.'

The sudden concern in his tone was nearly as unnerving as his prior harshness. Lifting her chin and eyelids simultaneously, Brandy faced him squarely, aware once again of Darcy crying softly beside her.

'I'm perfectly all right.' She wasn't. In fact, she actually felt sick to her stomach. 'Is this true, Darcy?' The tight rein with which she was controlling her emotions was reflected in her strained whisper.

'Yes.'

'But *why*?'

Even though Brandy had known what the answer would be, Darcy's sobbing admission drew the cry from her. Although they certainly did not live in luxury's lap, they had never really wanted for anything. If they had been starving and Darcy had been caught stealing a loaf of bread, Brandy would have been upset, but she would have understood. They were not starving, they were not even deprived, and all Brandy understood was that, in some way, she had failed her sister.

'That's what I'd like to know. Why?'

Brandy blinked and refocused on the hazel eyes, now intently studying her suddenly pale cheeks.

'I really do think you should sit down, Miss Styer,' Mitchell Waring urged with quiet forcefulness. Reaching out a large, broad hand at the end of a long, muscular arm, he curled blunt-tipped fingers around her arm to lead her to a chair. The contact sent a sensation not unlike an electric shock charging from her elbow to her shoulder, and down to her fingers. Startled, she jerked her arm away, then immediately felt foolish for overreacting.

'I ... I ... yes, I will,' she stammered in embarrassment. 'If you'll join me?' She had not missed the way his eyes had narrowed at her recoil from his touch and, feeling flustered and oddly confused, she made an attempt at covering her reaction by turning to draw Darcy to the wing-backed sofa that flanked the far wall.

'As you wish.' Mitchell Waring crossed the room and lowered his large frame into the easy chair facing the sofa with an agile grace unusual in a man so very tall. Settling back comfortably, he pinned her to the sofa with a disconcertingly direct stare.

'I realise this must be very upsetting for you, Miss Styer, but I hope you appreciate the fact that my having brought Darcy home is not my usual method of dealing with shoplifters.'

'I don't know.' Brandy shook her head in bafflement. 'What *is* your usual method?'

His lips twisted in a smile of disbelief. 'Either you take me for a fool, or you're incredibly naïve.' His sharp gaze judged her and, Brandy felt certain, found her sadly wanting. 'I usually press charges of theft.'

Brandy winced, as much from the cold, measured timbre of his tone as from the content of his words. She was not that naïve! No one was *that* naïve! She knew that were Darcy charged with theft, her name would very likely remain on record for the rest of her life. Darcy with a police record! The mere thought brought a frightened protest bursting through her stiff lips.

'But you're not going to do that ... are you?' Brandy held her breath and waited—and waited. His face expressionless, Mitchell Waring regarded her with clear, cool eyes for long, long moments.

'No,' he finally agreed, 'I'm not going to do that— this time. On questioning, Darcy swore to me that she's never done anything like this before.' His gaze sliced to the now dry-eyed but still trembling seventeen-year-old. 'Were you telling me the truth?'

'Yes, sir,' Darcy replied at once, if unsteadily. 'And I promise I'll never do anything like that again,' she vowed fervently. Hesitantly, she raised imploring eyes to Brandy. 'I ... I'm sorry, Brandy,' she whispered contritely.

'But why did you do it?' Brandy's cry held an equal measure of pain and anger. 'What did you think you had to have so badly you had to steal it to get it?'

Darcy blinked successfully against a fresh rush of tears and, her perfect white teeth digging into her lip, hung her head abjectly.

'A container of mascara.' The information came from the man sitting opposite Brandy, not from the girl beside her.

'What?'

The echo of Brandy's loud exclamation reverberated around the room.

'Exactly.' Mitchell Waring shook his head disgustedly. 'A lousy container of mascara that sells for under five dollars.'

Brandy understood his disgust, for, try as she might, she could not deny her own. She had knocked herself out over the last five years in an effort to emulate her parents in instilling honesty, morality, and

good value judgment into her younger sisters. That
she had obviously failed in her endeavours was bad
enough. Having that failure pointed out to her by way
of an inexpensive article of cosmetics was a pill too
bitter to swallow meekly. She exploded.

'For heaven's sake, Darcy, what got into you? You
have all kinds of cosmetics on your dresser, including
several different brands of mascara!' Hearing the rising
shrillness in her voice, Brandy forced herself to stop and
draw a calming breath. 'I want an explanation—at once!'

'You're not going to like it,' Darcy mumbled
tremulously.

'I don't like any of this,' Brandy snapped. 'Get on
with it.'

'Well . . .' Sure of the coming outburst, the teenager
hesitated, then rushed on, 'It's the latest . . . er . . .
kinda test with the group of girls I hang around with.
You know, like the boys play chicken-at-the-wheel on
the road?'

'Oh, good lord!' Brandy groaned.

'Wonderful!' Mitchell Waring grunted.

'Don't you see?' Darcy pleaded anxiously. 'It's a
test of courage. We all had to take at least one thing,
just to see if we could get away with it.'

'A test.' The sudden weariness that washed over
Brandy was reflected in her voice. Slumping tiredly
against the sofa's high back, she forced herself to face
the target of her sister's test. He was not looking at her
but staring at Darcy, his expression disdainful.
Somewhat fearful of what he might say to the girl,
Brandy rushed to forestall him. 'I want the names and
phone numbers of every one of the girls in your
group.'

'What for?' Darcy's head jerked up and she eyed
Brandy suspiciously.

'Because I am going to call their parents and tell them about this little test.'

'But you can't!'

'But I certainly can—and I will,' Brandy contradicted angrily. 'Parents have a silent agreement to keep each other informed about things like this.'

'But you're not my parent!'

'I'm the closest thing to one you're ever again going to know.' Brandy hated the harshness of her tone, but Darcy's protest had, possibly, caused the worst pain of all. She had tried so very, very hard.

'I'm not going to tell you,' Darcy grumbled, stubbornly. 'I'm no fink.'

'Darcy, I . . .'

'I think you may as well save your breath,' Mitchell Waring interrupted. 'Your sister may be mistakenly dishonest, but at least she's loyal—in a fashion.' With a fluid swiftness he rose to his feet and stood towering over her. 'As stated, I will not press charges—this time. Her employment is, naturally, terminated.'

'I do appreciate your consideration in bringing Darcy home, Mr Waring.' Controlling the urge to scramble to her feet, Brandy rose slowly. Faced from an upright position he didn't seem quite so intimidating. 'And I assure you there will be no next time.'

'I'm—I'm really sorry, Mr Waring.'

Brandy felt a rush of compassion for her sister. Everything about her reflected the fear Darcy felt for this imposing man. Brandy could only imagine what he had put Darcy through when he had confronted her for shoplifting. When had that first been? she wondered. Two hours ago? Three? She had to let Darcy escape.

'Darcy, go and bathe your eyes in cold water, then

go down and help your sisters with supper. I'll see Mr
Waring out.'

The speed with which Darcy obeyed made it
abundantly clear that she could not get away fast
enough. The sardonic smile that briefly curved
Mitchell Waring's lips made it equally clear he was
fully aware of the reason for Darcy's haste. Brandy
bristled at what she perceived to be a hint of cruelty in
that fleeting twitch of his lips.

'She's scared to death of you,' she accused heatedly.
'What did you do to her?'

'I administered an obviously much-needed tongue-
lashing.' Mitchell Waring's retort was followed by a
searing scrutiny of her person. 'Now, after observing
the domestic situation, I can better understand her
undisciplined behaviour.'

'What do you mean?' All the anger that had
subsided with the shock of learning about Darcy's
aborted attempt at shoplifting came storming back
with a force that shook her.

'Besides the three girls I've seen, are there any
others in your charge?' he counter-questioned.

'No.'

'And how long have you had guardianship?' One of
his elegantly winged eyebrows arched insolently.

Brandy became conscious of gritting her teeth when
her jaw began an aching protest. This had to be *the*
most arrogant, overbearing male she'd ever had the
misfortune to cross paths—or swords—with! Did he
really believe the present circumstances gave him the
right to give *her* the third degree?

'Five years.' Her answer came on a strangled note,
being pushed, as it was, through her clenched teeth.
'Why?'

'Why? You need ask?' His other brow joined its

counterpart on his forehead. 'It would immediately become apparent, to the most casual of onlookers, that you're much too young for the responsibility.'

'Too young?' Brandy's entire body went rigid. 'I'm twenty-five years old! What the hell do you mean—too young?'

'Are you really?' Cool hazel eyes studied her make-up-free face. 'Extraordinary! I'd have judged you to be around nineteen.' His lips twitched with the closest thing to a genuine smile Brandy had thus far witnessed. 'Nevertheless, you're still too young.'

Brandy quivered with indignation. The nerve of the beast!

'By what right do you make judgments of any kind?' she demanded in an outraged, choked squeak.

'In this case, by right of the injured party,' he retaliated coldly. '*I'm* the one who has been inconvenienced by the results of your immature guardianship.' His eyes raked her derisively. 'I dread to think of what kind of antics those two younger girls I caught a glimpse of downstairs might get up to in the future.'

'That's not fair!' Brandy cried in protest. 'You heard Darcy! It was a stupid teenage dare.'

'Which she went along with,' Mitchell Waring retorted. 'I can't help but wonder if the root cause of her apparent lack of ethical courage is a direct result of inadequate training.'

'And your children are perfect paragons of all the virtues, I suppose?' Brandy shouted defensively.

'As I'm unmarried, fatherhood is one of the . . . er . . . joys I have yet to experience,' he admitted smoothly.

Brandy's jaw dropped in sheer astonishment. Here she was, actually beginning to suffer pangs of guilt, only to find this clod was chastising her from a position of ignorance! New strength surged through her system, banishing the sensation of defeat she'd been feeling. The first order of business, she decided briskly, was to evict this arrogant man from *her* house.

'Yes, well, in that case, you're hardly in a position to talk, are you?' Brandy was rather pleased with the condescending tone she'd achieved. Her pleasure deepened when he stiffened.

'One does not necessarily have to *be* a parent to know if the job's being performed correctly.'

'Perhaps not,' Brandy agreed obligingly, then shot, 'But it does help.' Before he could contradict her, she went on quickly, 'I *am* grateful to you for bringing Darcy home, Mr Waring, and I *do* understand that you're a busy man.' She paused for a fleeting second, then nudged, very gently, 'I wouldn't want to keep you.'

CHAPTER TWO

WHEN Brandy finally closed the door after Mitchell Waring some fifteen minutes later, she leaned back against it, closing her eyes on a long sigh of relief.

After a brief narrow-eyed pause, he had taken her hint and walked out of the living room and down the stairs, Brandy at his heels. At the bottom of the stairs she had caught back a groan of dismay when, instead of moving to the door, he turned and strolled into her shop.

Moving slowly, without speaking, he had examined the stock displayed on the shelves and centre counter, his gaze lingering on an intricately carved piece Brandy was particularly proud of. He had been so quiet that when he spoke she had jerked to attention, even though his voice was low.

'Exquisite.'

'Th—Thank you.'

Brandy had been unnerved and surprised at the tremor of uncertainty that had laced her automatic response. Only by a concentrated effort had she managed a steady tone as she had replied to his subsequent queries.

'You make all the candles displayed here?'

'Yes.'

'Do your sisters help?'

'Occasionally, at the busiest times of the year— Christmas and Easter.'

'Incredible.' He'd given a brief shake of his head, then his gaze had returned to her pride and joy. 'This one is exceptionally beautiful. How did you learn to do that?'

'Trial and error.'

The glance he had shot at her held both admiration and respect.

'Amazing!'

The amazing thing, to Brandy, had been his unqualified appreciation, for, by and large, her male customers rarely seemed to consider the artistry of her work.

Now, Mitchell Waring at last having taken his leave, Brandy leaned against the solid support of the door, her breathing inexplicably uneven. Something about that large man made her feel very young and vulnerable. Brandy did not like the feeling one bit.

'Supper's on the table, Brand.'

Bev's call shattered Brandy's trancelike bemusement and with a mental shake she dismissed her confusing thoughts about the over-confident, arrogant Mr Mitchell Waring.

'Coming!'

As she acknowledged Bev's call she pushed herself erect and started through the shop, pausing moment- arily as her gaze brushed the candle that had received Mitchell Waring's close scrutiny. Then, quickening her pace, she headed for the kitchen.

Long after the house had grown quiet that night Brandy lay restless and wakeful.

The family conclave, concerning Darcy's fall from grace, that had been held around the supper table had left her feeling exhausted and uncharacteristically weepy.

Although she had defended Darcy's action to Mitchell Waring as a teenage dare, Brandy considered it her duty as guardian to administer a lecture on honesty.

Even while her parents were alive they had always been a close family. After the death of their parents and seven-year-old brother, in the crash of a small plane, the four surviving Styers had drawn even more tightly together. Their very closeness had been a supporting factor for Brandy when, after the initial shock had worn off, she had taken on the responsibility of head of the house.

Tonight, for the very first time, Brandy had been made to feel shut out. Closer in age, her three younger sisters had seemingly closed ranks against her.

'It's no big thing, you know,' Bev had shrugged her shoulders unconcernedly. 'Most kids try it at least once, just to see if they can get away with it.'

Which, of course, had made Brandy wonder, worriedly, if Bev herself had had a go at it.

'I can't see why you're getting yourself in such an uproar about it.' Karen had jumped in on the side of the defence. 'It's not as if Darcy's a criminal or something.'

Frustrated by her inability to impress upon them the seriousness of the incident, Brandy had seized on Karen's assertion.

'I know that. But don't you understand that she could have had the status of a criminal? Mr Waring was furious; and rightly so. If he'd followed his usual procedure and turned her in Darcy would now have a permanent record.'

'But he didn't do that,' Karen argued. 'So why get all bent out of shape?'

Brandy had already begun to taste defeat. Bev had simply put a period to the end of the argument.

'Yeah, it was pretty neat of him not to yelp for the law,' Bev had opined, wonderingly. 'Old man Waring must be an all-right guy.'

It was hours now since Brandy had winced at Bev's less then elegant language, yet it was Bev's final phrase her restless mind settled on. Old man Waring? The man couldn't be more than thirty-six or seven. Of course, to a fourteen-year-old, the mid-thirties must seem like a very advanced age. Strangely enough, Brandy herself had felt an intimidating sensation, as if dealing with an older, authoritarian figure.

Of course, the size of him was intimidating. Lord, he was big! Yet she had met other men of equal stature, or close to it, and had not felt overly impressed, and not at all overwhelmed. No, it was more then the number of inches required to measure his length.

Staring at the pale blue of the ceiling in the darkened room, Brandy formed a mental image of Mitchell Waring. A chill crept over her skin as she pictured his cool, direct, hazel-eyed stare. Those eyes, set into his harshly cast, forbidding face, were far more intimidating then mere size.

In the privacy of her bedroom, in the confines of her own head, Brandy came to the reluctant conclusion that Mitchell Waring scared the hell out of her; she hoped she would never have to encounter him again.

During the rest of that week Brandy was visited, at odd hours of the day and night, by sharp, precise images of Mitchell Waring. Suddenly without warning, whether she was pouring wax, or carving, or forming the small, individual wax circles into the petals that made up the rose candles that were so popular with her customers, a picture of him would flash through her mind. By Friday her memory was saturated with a surface knowledge of him. The curve of his lips, the thrust of his jaw, his large, broad hands, his long, muscular legs—all were familiar to her. At one point Brandy thought she could even smell the sharp, tangy scent of his aftershave splash-on. Try as she might to banish these strange flashes they continued, and with each successive one she became more resentful of him.

On the home front, things were back to normal.

Darcy had come to Brandy's bedroom on Tuesday night to tell her she had had a talk with her friends and they had prudently decided to forgo their current version of I-dare-you. Karen was, as always, busy with her studies—and making believe she was uninterested in the innocent advances of a boy in her history class. Bev was on the go from the moment she sprang out of bed in the morning till she fell back into it at night.

By silent agreement the subject of Darcy's step out of line was not raised again.

Saturday brought a flurry of customers, a very light flurry, and, late in the afternoon, one Mitchell Waring. Brandy was making change for a rather talkative but nice elderly lady and didn't even look up at the sound of the door being opened and closed.

When, after answering another of the woman's seemingly endless supply of questions concerning her handiwork, Brandy did glance away, her gaze collided with his steady hazel stare.

He was attired much the same as he had been the previous Monday in a conservative, excellently cut three-piece suit, pristine white shirt and subdued tie, and for a tiny instant Brandy had the uncanny sensation her imagination had gone completely haywire and conjured him up.

Her own gasp of dismay was overshadowed and covered by the exclamation of the chatty senior citizen.

'Good heavens!' that gentle lady gasped as she turned towards the door and caught sight of him. 'You *are* a big one, aren't you?'

'Yes,' he answered simply, an amused smile revealing even, white teeth.

Brightly alert, birdlike dark eyes twinkled back at him out of Miss Senior Citizen's parchment-like face.

'Good-looking, too,' she chirped, also birdlike.

Good-looking? Brandy thought blankly. Mitchell Waring? Obviously the old dear had a vision problem.

His soft, appreciative chuckle scattered Brandy's wondering thoughts and she watched as, with a courtly grace, he bowed from the waist. As he straightened he captured one delicately wrinkled, fragile hand with his and bestowed a gentle kiss on the fingers while murmuring, 'What a delightfully charming liar you are, but I do thank you, beautiful lady.'

'Oh, my,' that 'beautiful lady' fluttered. 'I'd better get out of here before my head is well and truly turned!' Turning her bright-eyed gaze back to Brandy, she cautioned, 'Be careful, dear, this one knows his way around the ladies!'

Brandy's smile did justice to her talent for concealment. Behind the parody of her lip motion she was a mass of conflicting emotions. The front-runner of her feelings was annoyance. She had hoped never to lay eyes on him again; yet here he was, big as a mountain, and twice as hard to ignore.

Behind her annoyance, but crowding close, lurked the nagging worry, had he changed his mind about reporting Darcy to the authorities?

In the background, but being felt just the same, simmered an odd mixture of fear and resentment. Her emotions seemed to be trying to warn her that this man was a threat to her, personally, even while her reasoning faculties insisted that her fears were groundless.

'Alone at last!'

Mitchell Waring's softly drawled assertion jerked Brandy out of her introspection and into the realisation that her twittering customer had left the store. When had she made her departure? Just now? Five minutes ago? Had he been watching her, searching for a clue to her reaction at his sudden appearance? Feeling exposed, Brandy rushed into speech.

'Hardly alone,' she hastened to correct him. 'All three of my sisters are here'—she moved her hand to encompass the building—'somewhere.'

'Pity.' His drawling, uninterested tone belied the sentiment and, perversely, Brandy bristled.

'For whom?' she drawled back insultingly.

'Perhaps for both of us,' he rejoined silkily, his eyes beginning to gleam wickedly.

Telling herself those hazel depths were merely reflecting the glow from the numerous candles burning away steadily in the room, Brandy ordered her lips into a dismissive smile.

'I seriously doubt it.' She felt satisfaction at the toss-away tone she'd achieved. Slicing a furtive glance at the large sunburst clock on the wall behind the service counter, she smothered a sigh of relief. It was eight minutes shy of her five o'clock closing time and, as she had a dinner date at seven, her first order of business was to get rid of this over-large, overbearing man. That thought in mind, she met his cool, hazel-eyed stare head-on.

'As I assume you didn't drop by simply to browse, what can I do for you, Mr Waring?'

Even though the lighted candles in the shop

continued to flicker evenly, a flame leaped briefly in those hazel depths.

'You could do all manner of things for me—some day,' he suggested in a deep drawl, then, with lightning speed, his tone became brisk. 'As for this minute, you're correct—I didn't stop by to browse. I had two reasons for dropping by. First: I need a hostess gift for this evening. As a rule I send flowers or take candy or wine,' he explained blandly. 'My hostess this evening is a woman of discerning taste, and I know she would appreciate the beauty and workmanship in the candle I admired on Monday. I stopped in to purchase it, or one similar if you'd sold it.' His gaze shifted back to the object in question. 'As you obviously haven't sold it, I'll have it.'

'Very well.' Brandy moved from her relatively safe position behind the service counter to collect the piece she had lavished so much time on in its creation, wondering if he'd noticed its cost, handwritten on a tiny price tag. The price posted was the very reason she had not sold it. There had been several customers interested in it, but not to the tune of the amount she had decided the work deserved.

Handling the candle carefully, she carried it into her workroom, irritation prickling her nerves when she heard him follow her. The man certainly didn't lack for gall! Now he was invading her work area!

Her movements swift, competent, she boxed and wrapped her prize, finishing it off with a large gold bow, fully conscious of his progress as he examined her work in its various degrees of completeness.

'Very nice,' he complimented her efforts as she put the finishing touches to the gold bow.

'Thank you.' Brandy's tone held no thrill of

accomplishment. 'Would you like to choose a gift card?'

He was shaking his head before she had completed the question. 'That won't be necessary, thank you.'

'All right.' Sliding the package towards him, she quoted the price, watching sharply for his reaction. There was none.

His expression bland, he nodded briefly and reached for his wallet, then counted out bills sufficient to cover the cost.

Her uppermost thought being to evict him from the premises, Brandy counted the change quickly. Carefully not touching him, she placed the change in his palm and nudged, pointedly. 'You said you had two reasons for stopping by?'

'Yes.' His twitching lips acknowledged her avoidance of any personal contact. 'I was wondering how Darcy was getting along.'

Why? The one word question sprang to her lips, but resentfully, Brandy refused to voice it. In bringing Darcy home to her on Monday he had, in effect, washed his hands of the matter—hadn't he? Yes, he had, she decided angrily. He had no right to ask questions now! Firmly determined she would answer no further questions, she nevertheless condescended to reply to the one he'd asked.

'Darcy is doing very well, th . . .'

That was as far as she got, for at that moment Darcy's voice preceded her into the room.

'Brandy, it's after five, haven't you closed the shop yet? I thought . . .' at the sight of her former employer her voice faltered to a whispering thread, 'you had a date?'

Brandy's feeling of resentment deepened as she saw her sister's eyes widen with fear and the colour seep out of her face. Now, for Darcy's sake as well as her own, she had to get rid of him.

'I do have a date.' Even though her answer was aimed at Darcy, Brandy looked directly at Mitchell Waring. 'If there's nothing else?'

'But there is,' he insisted, if softly. His gaze sliced to the frightened seventeen-year-old. 'There's nothing to be afraid of, Darcy.' His gentle assurance revealed awareness of the girl's near-panic state. 'I was wondering if you'd found other employment.'

'N—no,' Darcy whispered, her mesmerised stare never leaving his face.

'Then I think we have something to discuss.' Cocking his head, he arched one dark, elegantly winged brow at Brandy. 'Please, don't let me keep you from closing your shop and getting ready for your date. My business is with Darcy.' Ignoring her tiny gasp at his dismissive tone, he levelled a charmingly breathtaking smile on Darcy. 'Is there somewhere we could talk?'

Fighting a sudden urge to slap his smiling face, Brandy reached the conclusion that there was no way she would leave Darcy alone with this mountain posing as a man.

'Oh, you couldn't keep me from *anything*, Mr Waring.' She favoured him with the most sickeningly sweet smile she could form with her lips. 'I was going to have a cup of coffee before getting ready, anyway,' she lied without batting an eyelash. Bestowing a genuine smile on her sister, she directed, 'Show Mr Waring into the kitchen while I lock up, honey. I'll be with you in a moment.'

When she went into the kitchen after securing the shop for the night, Brandy was both shocked and surprised to find Darcy laughing easily with Mitchell

Waring. What could possibly have occurred in the few minutes she'd been out of their company to have changed Darcy so? she wondered confusedly. Darcy's formerly fear-ridden eyes were now dancing with laughter! What could he have said to cause such a drastic change in her?

Hesitating on the threshold, Brandy made a concentrated effort at concealing the irritation that rippled through her at the sight of them. 'Have I missed something?' she asked with patently false lightness.

'Nothing of any importance.'

Looking far too relaxed as he lounged precariously on a kitchen chair, Mitchell Waring didn't even bother to glance at her. Although she could not be certain, Brandy thought she saw him wink conspiratorially at Darcy.

Annoyed beyond all reason, she strode into the room. Coffee was perking merrily away in the electric pot and, even though she really didn't want any, she went to the cabinet where the cups were housed.

'Will you have a cup of coffee, Mr Waring?'

Brandy's hand hovered at the cup shelf, waiting for him to reply to Darcy's invitation, hoping he'd say no, state his business and go. But her hopes were in vain.

'Yes, thank you.'

Turned to the cabinet, Brandy couldn't see his expression, yet his sardonic inflection left her in little doubt that he had correctly interpreted her desire to see the back of him. With lightning swiftness the realisation struck her that this man was deliberately trying to provoke her! Why he should want to annoy her she had no idea, but, in that second, she decided to show him that two could play at that game.

Smiling serenely, Brandy filled two cups with the

aromatic brew and placed them on the table. Sitting down opposite him, she nodded her thanks to Darcy for providing a jug of cream and a bowl of sugar.

'Now, Mr Waring, you said there was something you wanted to discuss with Darcy?' Brandy glanced pointedly at the clock, then back to him, a strange thrill piercing her as his lids lowered over his suddenly glittering eyes. Her silent reference to the time had annoyed him! Chalk one up for me, she thought smugly.

'That's right.' His tone was soft, warning soft. Again that odd thrill pierced Brandy. 'And, since my business *is* with Darcy, don't let me keep you, Miss Styer.' His lids lifted fractionally to reveal the challenge gleaming in his eyes.

'Oh, believe me,' her tone as soft as his, Brandy accepted his visual challenge, 'you could never *keep* me, Mr Waring.'

An indefinable something flickered in his eyes before his lids came down again.

'Oh, I think I could, Brandy,' he taunted her with the use of her first name. 'Yes, I think I could—very easily.'

Though Mitchell Waring's eyes held her captive, Brandy was fully aware of Darcy's blank look of confusion as her gaze shifted back and forth between them. Very obviously Darcy felt *something* was taking place here that she didn't understand. Brandy knew exactly how Darcy felt; *she* didn't quite understand what was going on! One thing was clear as an unpolluted stream; their exchange had had nothing whatever to do with Darcy.

Beginning to feel she was on very shaky ground, Brandy sidestepped warily. 'Have you changed your mind about reporting Darcy?'

The seventeen-year-old's gasp of fright was heard, and ignored by the antagonists. Brandy now knew that was not the reason for his visit. Mitchell Waring knew Brandy knew—he answered just the same.

'No.' A tiny smile acknowleged Darcy's sigh of relief, but his gaze remained locked on Brandy. 'As a matter of fact, I came to offer her other employment.'

'At one of your stores!' Brandy didn't bother to conceal her astonishment. However, she did manage to hide her dismay at the idea—at least she thought she had. The amusement that flashed across his strong features instilled doubt.

'No, Brandy, not at one of my stores.' His patient tone set her teeth on edge.

'Where, then?' she gritted.

'Hey!' Darcy yelped before he could answer. 'Since I'm the one involved here, don't you think you should be talking to me?' As she made her appeal, Darcy placed her hand on Mitchell Waring's sleeve. The stab of annoyance that shot through her at the sight of Darcy's slender hand on his arm stunned her.

Why should seeing her sister touch this man annoy her? As Brandy could come up with no logical explanation to her own question, she forced her attention to his answer to Darcy.

'You're right, of course.' His long, broad hand covered Darcy's, and Brandy had to clamp her teeth together to keep from protesting aloud.

What was wrong with her? Brandy squirmed in her chair and again forced herself to concentrate on what he was saying.

'You are the one involved here, and I'll talk to you—on one condition.' He smiled beguilingly, prompting a shy smile in return from Darcy, and a sensation of near pain in Brandy.

'What condition?' Darcy asked the question that itched on the tip of Brandy's tongue.

'That you drop the Mr Waring business and call me Mitch.'

Darcy's eyes flew wide, then she giggled. 'Okay, Mitch, it's a deal. Now, talk to me.' Her eyelashes swept down and then up again as a sweet smile curved her tender young lips.

Silently watchful, beginning to feel invisible, Brandy widened her eyes in sheer astonishment. Darcy was actually daring to flirt with the arrogantly formidable man facing her!

Mitchell Waring's bark of delighted laughter rocketed through Brandy. Oh, yes, she thought, shakily, this man was formidable in more ways than one!

His anger had the power to freeze whoever it was directed at, Brandy knew, for she had been the unfortunate recipient of it. In turn, his gentleness thawed, she also knew, for she had observed the effect on Darcy. Now, to her discomfort, she knew that the sound of his laughter absolutely melted, for she could feel her own body juices quickening into a flash-flood. Formidable indeed!

Scrupulously controlling her reaction to the disarming quality of his amusement, Brandy composed her features into cool disdain. Unsure of just how long she would be able to maintain her composure, she wished, fervently, that he would state his reason for stopping and take his leave.

As if he could monitor her thoughts, he swung his amusement-brightened eyes to hers, one eyebrow arching insolently at the cold front she presented to him. He held her gaze relentlessly for several long seconds, then, outrageously, he slowly lowered one lid.

Sheer, unreasoning fury, tinged equally with unreasoned fear, blazed through Brandy. How dared he treat her in the same manner he'd used on Darcy! *She* was no impressionable, giddy seventeen-year-old!

Brandy was on the verge of exploding all over the kitchen when, luckily, the seventeen-year-old in question shattered the sudden stillness in the air.

'Well, come on, Mitch,' Darcy wailed. 'Don't keep me in suspense! What's the deal?'

His lips still twitching with his baffling inner amusement, Mitchell Waring finally released his visual hold on Brandy and turned to the girl. 'The deal is the offer of a part-time position in the office of a friend of mine.' He was all seriousness now. 'If you're interested. Are you?'

'*If* I'm interested?' Darcy fairly yelped. 'Of course I'm interested! What kind of job is it? What kind of office?'

'An insurance office,' he answered the latter first. 'My friend George Detrick needs someone part-time to answer the phone, do some file work, and——' he paused, then added, consideringly, 'Do you type at all?'

'Yes.' Darcy nodded enthusiastically. 'I'm not all that fast,' she admitted. 'But I am pretty accurate,' she tacked on hopefully.

'Good enough,' he decided. 'You can always build speed. Okay, I told George I'd have a talk with you and, if you were interested, have you call him to discuss the details.' Reaching into his pocket, he withdrew a small white business card and handed it to Darcy. 'George said you could reach him at this number till six-thirty.'

Darcy's eyes flew to the butcher block wall clock, which read five past six. Brandy's glance followed and when she saw the time, her lips tightened against emitting a groan. She was really going to be rushed if she was to be ready when her date arrived.

Once again Mitchell Waring, unnervingly, seemed to read her mind, for, his lips curving sardonically, he drained his cup and got lighly to his feet and, once again, his eyes captured Brandy's.

'I've taken up enough of your time,' he murmured before turning back to Darcy. 'Good luck with George.'

'Thank you for everything, Mr——' Darcy hesitated when he frowned, then, grinning, she went on, 'Mitch. You're a real sweetheart!'

Brandy's soft, shocked gasp went unheard as it was covered by his chuckle and an exclamation that came from the enclosed back stairway that ran to the second floor.

'Gee, it's too bad this Mr Detrick doesn't need two girls!'

Although three heads swivelled simultaneously, Brandy was the first one to speak. 'Karen! Since when have you been practising the art of eavesdropping?'

'I wasn't eavesdropping,' Karen denied Brandy's charge. 'At least, I didn't mean to,' she qualified, blushing scarlet. 'I didn't even know anyone was down here till I got to the bottom of the stairs, and then——' she shrugged, 'well, I didn't want to interrupt.'

'No harm done.' Mitchell Waring excused Karen smoothly, even as Brandy opened her mouth to scold. 'You're also looking for work?' he asked the red-faced girl gently.

'Yes, sir,' Karen nodded.

'How old are you?'

'Fifteen . . . and a half.'

The smile of beguilement was back in place. 'It

limits the possibilities, but would you be interested in baby-sitting?'

'Anything that will give me some spending money,' Karen avowed, somewhat dramatically. 'Even house-work!'

'Hmm,' Mitchell Waring grinned in appreciation of her performance. 'Okay, kid,' he chuckled, 'I'll ask around and get back to you.'

'Will you?' Karen squealed, round-eyed. 'Do you mean it?'

'As I've already told your sister, youngster,' he admonished softly, 'I always mean what I say.'

'Super!' Karen cried. 'Thanks, Mr Waring.'

'Mitch,' he grinned.

Stationed at the archway into her workroom, the last vestiges of her patience disintegrating, Brandy slowly began counting to ten. Mitchell Waring bade the two girls 'so long' when she reached seven, and strode by her on the count of nine.

'I hope the candle gives satisfaction,' Brandy murmured as pleasantly as she possibly could when he paused to scoop up the elegantly bowed package.

'I'm sure it will,' he drawled, his long stride outdistancing her on their trek to the front door. 'I'll be in touch.' When her only response was a querying lift of her brows, he sighed, exaggeratedly. 'If I hear of employment suitable for Karen,' he reminded her patiently.

'Oh!' Now Brandy felt her own cheeks grow pink. 'Yes, of course. Thank you, and good evening, Mr Waring.'

Closing his eyes briefly, he sighed again before repeating for the third time, 'Mitch.'

No way in hell! Brandy surprised herself with her own emphatic thought. Outwardly, she managed a small smile instead of a reply.

Finally. Finally. Finally. The chant revolved in Brandy's head as she closed the door. For a minute there she had been afraid he would not budge until she'd pandered to his vanity by saying his name aloud.

No, thank you, *Mr Waring*. No way in hell, she promised herself as she dashed up the front stairs to get ready for her date.

CHAPTER THREE

FORGOING her desire for a long soaking bath, Brandy hurried through her shower and shampooing to give herself more time to blow-dry her hair into soft, loose curls before carefully applying her make-up.

At five minutes before seven, she stood in front of her mirror to cast her glance over her reflection in a final inspection. She had wanted to look especially nice for this date and, considering her lack of fussing time, she had succeeded fairly well.

Her long-sleeved, high-collared dress of a finely woven, soft wool hugged her body lovingly to the waistline. Below the narrow, supple leather belt, the skirt belled gently to swirl around her slender legs when she walked. The rich cranberry colour of the garment lent a soft, reflected glow to her lightly blushed cheeks. The classic simplicity of the dress was enhanced by a two-inch-wide ruffle of ivory lace at her throat and wrists. The slim-heeled sling-backs and small clutch bag were soft leather in a corresponding ivory tone. Her finely textured fair skin gleamed pearly-hued through a delicately applied foundation, and her soft grey eyes were highlighted by a touch of mascara and eye shadow.

Her critical perusal completed, Brandy nodded in approval at the lovely image staring back at her. Brandy was not in the least conceited about her above-average good looks; she was also not blind. She had realized at an early age that she was pleasing to look at, and she accepted her attractiveness gratefully.

A light tap on her bedroom door ended her inspection period.

'Brandy, Jason's here,' Bev called through the door.

'Coming!' Brandy called back, crossing the room to her closet to remove her one real indulgence of the previous five years. Two winters ago, fighting her conscience every inch of the way, she had succumbed to the lure of *the* coat.

Of smoothest cashmere, its style timeless, the coat was the one luxury Brandy had allowed herself. On the rare occasions she deemed important enough to wear it, a thrill of near-sensual pleasure invariably feathered her skin as she snuggled into the richness of the material.

Draping the coat carefully over one arm, she left her bedroom and walked along the hall to the living room, a warm welcoming smile on her freshly glossed lips. Before she had stepped into the room Jason Carstairs was on his feet, his soft brown eyes warm with appreciation of her appearance.

'You look beautiful, as usual,' he put into words the message his eyes had already telegraphed.

Brandy's smile deepened and her low, infectious laugh floated across the room to him. 'You're a man of discerning taste, Mr Carstairs,' she teased, relinquishing her coat into his hands. 'And I do thank you.'

Helping her into her coat, he lowered his head close to hers. 'And you have all the makings of a first-rate tease, which, I suspect, will some day get you into trouble—male trouble.'

The touch of his breath as it ruffled the hair near her ear was rather pleasing and, arching her head, Brandy gazed at him with sparkling grey eyes. 'I have yet to run across a man who can give me trouble.'

The moment the statement was out of her mouth a

picture of a large man careened through her mind, sending a thrill of apprehension straight down her spine.

'Oh, an independent tease, are you?' Jason's voice seemed to come from a distance.

'Yes.' The hesitant, whispery sound of her voice shocked Brandy into alertness. A spark of anger stiffened her back, banishing the apprehension.

'Yes.' She repeated, far more firmly, 'I'm *very* independent.'

'Okay, I'm convinced.'

Brandy had not even been aware of his hands resting on her shoulders until he lifted them in a sign of surrender and backed away in mock fear. 'You don't have to growl at me.' Giving up the pretence, he laughed. 'But I must admit I like you much better as a tease!'

Suddenly conscious of three pairs of eyes unashamedly watching the byplay between Jason and her, Brandy moved away from him to face her sisters.

Bev, sitting cross-legged on the floor by a small stereo unit, earphones clamped to her head, favoured her eldest sister with her engaging devil grin.

Karen, the serious student, was curled into a corner of the sofa, a textbook in her lap. Karen didn't grin, or even smile. Her sombre grey eyes regarded Brandy thoughtfully. For reasons Brandy could not fathom, Karen did not particularly like Jason Carstairs.

Darcy—referred to by Bev as the telephone freak— sat by that instrument, impatiently waiting, Brandy knew, for her to leave so that she could get to the exciting business of calling her friends to tell them about her newly acquired job.

In the face of their pained expressions, Brandy went through her usual lecture of no arguing among themselves, no opening the door to strangers, and exactly where she was going in case they should have to reach her—none of which calamities had ever materialised.

'You treat them like babies, and they're not any more.' Jason's tone held a definite edge of annoyance as he slid behind the wheel of his car on to the seat beside her. 'Isn't it time you let them grow up?' The slamming of his door added emphasis to his harshly voiced question.

Startled, Brandy turned to stare at him in shocked surprise. After bidding the girls a quiet 'good evening' Jason had remained silent as he followed her down the front stairway, out of the door, and along the sidewalk to where he had parked his flashy-looking, fire engine red stingray. His attack was all the more unnerving for its very suddenness.

'But they're still teenagers!' Brandy exclaimed defensively. 'And I *am* responsible for them, you know.'

'Only too well!' he snorted in exasperation. 'We can't go anywhere without leaving a phone number, or place name, or address, for God's sake!'

'Is that such an imposition?' Brandy chided softly, repressing the urge to upbraid him.

'Well, it sure as hell doesn't leave much leeway for spontaneity,' Jason shot back. 'Good grief, I've been under more strictures since I began dating you than I ever was while I still lived at home! I feel as if my movements are all monitored, and I don't like it.'

Brandy's sigh, halfway through his tirade, went unheard by the irate man beside her. Although his words were different, his tune was a very familiar one to Brandy.

How many times, she asked herself sadly, had she

heard this refrain over the last few years? Jason's melody was merely another variation on the now familiar song of complaint, whose leading strain was invariably centred on her lack of freedom.

As Brandy had never felt encumbered by the 'bondage' of her guardianship, she was invariably angered by the orchestration of the charge. This time was no exception.

'Might I suggest that the answer to your problem is obvious?' Brandy was long past tiptoeing around this particular bone of contention; she had lost count of the number of times she'd been forced to gnaw on it. 'If you feel the "strictures" surrounding your companion are too confining, you have simply to change the company you keep.'

A dead silence filled the car's small interior while Jason digested her stinging, if somewhat pompous-sounding, advice.

During that silence, Brandy sat with deceptive outward composure. Inside, she was a seething mass of conflicting emotions, uppermost of which was despair. Oh, there were anger, rebellion, and frustration in plenty, but the overriding emotion was simple despair. The sad part was, she was almost used to it.

How many times had she been through this scene of disgruntlement? Brandy mentally ticked off the list of her previous male escorts' names.

First there had been Keith Richards. That young man had voiced his displeasure concerning her role of surrogate mother on their tenth and last date. After Keith had come a slightly cocky yet breathtakingly handsome young lion named Mike Casey. Beautiful Mike had contained himself for three whole months of bi-weekly dating before exploding and spewing his ire. Charles Schoffer had followed Mike. A quiet,

easygoing man, Charles had hurt her the most by his
defection, possibly because she had expected more of
him.

All of them had claimed love for her. All of them
had mentioned marriage, if vaguely. All of them had,
in the end, made it clear that they wanted her, not her
family. When asked, and Brandy did ask, forcefully
and angrily, what exactly she was to do with her
sisters, they had all answered more or less the same.
What it had amounted to was: Who cares?

To one after the other, Brandy had politely but
firmly pointed out the direction to the door. Now
Jason had added his noise to the cacophony created by
his predecessors. Would she, she wondered, soon be
showing him the door as well?

'Are you saying you wouldn't give a damn if I *did*
change companions?'

The angry voice from beside her jerked Brandy out
of her withdrawn musing. Glancing up, she blinked
with surprise. They were very near to the restaurant
where Jason had made reservations for dinner, and she
had not even been aware he'd set the car in motion!

'You started this, Jason,' she reminded him by way
of an answer. 'Are you, in this obscure way, trying to
tell me something?'

'No!' Jason's denial came fast and loud. 'You know
how I feel about you, Brandy.'

Did she? She had thought ... but then she had
thought she knew with Keith, and Mike, and
especially Charles. She had not been 'in love' with any
of them, but she had been teetering on the brink.
Subsequently, she had been playing it cool with Jason.
Thrice burned leaves one very, very wary.

Jason swore softly when she failed to respond.
'Dammit, Brandy, you're driving me crazy! You ...'

he broke off abruptly as they reached the restaurant, concentrating on manoeuvring the sports car very carefully into a parking slot on the crowded lot. The moment the car was stationary he pushed open his door.

'I need a drink,' he informed her in a tone heavy with petulance. 'Let's shelve this discussion till after dinner.'

Even though her appetite had diminished greatly since she had got into the car, Brandy, suddenly weary, quietly agreed to his request.

The understated elegance of the restaurant's décor, the subdued lighting, the low hum of conversation, and the quiet, efficient service by the staff all had a soothing, relaxing effect on Brandy's thoroughly jangled nervous system.

All things considered, she decided tiredly, taking a tentative taste of her French onion soup, it had been one teeth-grinding week. That thought instantly produced a sharp image of a very tall, very arrogant takeover man; her spoon faltered en route to her mouth.

'You don't like the soup?' Jason's question mercifully banished her too clearly defined mental image of Mitchell Waring.

'It's delicious,' she hurriedly assured him. 'But it's also very hot.'

Satisfied with her reply, Jason launched into a recital of the humorous goof-ups that had occurred during the business trip he'd been on the previous week, and within minutes he had Brandy gasping with laughter.

By the time they left the congenial atmosphere of the restaurant all the earlier strain between them had dissolved and they were talking comfortably together.

Replete with her excellent dinner and mellow from the wine that had accompanied it, Brandy rested her head against the car seat, eyes closed, humming along with the ballad Barry Manilow was singing via the tape-deck. When the car came to a stop she lifted a hand to cover a yawn and slowly opened her eyes. 'Where are we?' she murmured, still dreamy with the effects of the romantic music.

'My place.'

Instantly alert, Brandy sat up in her seat, her eyes reproachful as she swung her startled gaze to his. 'Jason, you know . . .'

'Yes, I know,' his exasperated voice cut across her protest. 'You've consistently refused to as much as enter my apartment, but we've got to talk, in private, and we sure as hell can't have any privacy at your place. For God's sake, Brandy, you're twenty-five years old,' he expostulated heatedly. 'Well past the age of being terrified of going into a bachelor apartment. Come on,' he coaxed. 'You have to grow up some time.'

As she had considered herself quite grown up for some five years now, his last barb effectively demolished the argument Brandy had been busy marshalling. Making an unusual snap decision, she flung open the door and, stepping on to the pavement, snapped, 'All right, let's go and get this . . . discussion over with.'

The moment they stepped into his apartment Brandy knew her snap decision had been a mistake. After closing the door Jason leaned back against it and reached out to grasp her arms, pulling her off balance so that she literally fell into his arms.

'Jason, don't . . .'

Her admonition was smothered by the insistent

pressure of his mouth on hers. Brandy didn't fight him, but she didn't join him either. When her lack of response registered, Jason released her lips enough to plead, tritely, 'Brandy, please, I've been waiting all week for this.'

'I . . . I have to call home.' Arching her head back, Brandy raised her hands to push against his chest.

'For God's sake!' he groaned disgustedly. 'It's only ten-thirty.'

'But I told the kids we'd be going to the club after the restaurant.' Brandy sighed. 'Don't you see? If something came up they wouldn't know where to reach me. I must let them know where I am.'

'That's exactly what I was talking about earlier,' his tone was heavy with frustration. 'You have to account for every second you're away from the house.'

'I don't have to account to anyone!' Brandy exclaimed in protest.

'Well, I'd like to know what you call it,' Jason grumbled.

'Being responsible,' Brandy snapped impatiently. 'They're teenage girls, and when I'm away I want them to be able to reach me if necessary. I see nothing hard to understand about that!' Shrugging out of his hold, she straightened and, hands planted aggressively on her enticingly rounded hips, stared at him out of stormy grey eyes.

'The fact of the matter is,' she went on stiffly, 'I'm not "free" in the sense you are. I accept that.' She bit back another sigh of weariness. How often had she ploughed through this explanation? More tiring still— how many more times would she have to trudge along the same furrow? 'I wasn't forced into this guardianship, Jason. I fought for it, fully cognisant of the personal limitations it would entail.'

'Okay, okay, I get the picture.' Jason held his hands up in the air. 'You can step off your soapbox.' His lips twisted. 'Go and make your damn duty call.'

It was over in that moment. Whatever they had had going for them, however nebulous, was gone with his dismissive order. Brandy knew it, and Jason confirmed it.

'I had thought that maybe . . . you and I could get together.' Pushing himself away from the door, he grasped her arms. 'But there's no way I'm going to take on a ready-made family; not many men would.'

Tell me about it. Brandy didn't even bother voicing the thought. What would be the point? No one knew better than she that what he'd said was true. She'd heard basically the same feelings expressed from three other very different men.

'We could still have some fun.'

Brandy's eyes flickered to his face at the change in his tone. A very attractive face it was too. A sigh of regret shivered through her soft lips as she watched that face draw closer to her own.

His kiss began as a soft farewell salute, but quickly changed into a demand for capitulation. His arms held her immobile while his lips ravaged hers brutally. Brandy tasted her own blood and froze, a myriad emotions churning her stomach into nausea.

Sheer outrage quickly consumed all other emotions. How dared he! He had, only moments ago, figuratively washed his hands of her. Yet now his devouring mouth and roving hands were suggesting blatantly that they make their last encounter a physical one.

Did he actually believe he was so irresistible she would give up her innocence to him as a parting gift? No, of course he didn't, she thought instinctively. She was twenty-five. Very probably he simply never considered the remote possibility *of* her innocence!

Damn all men!

On the heels of the mental indictment Brandy's hands came up to push him away. Damn their arrogance and conceit! With the strength born of fury, she tore loose from his grasping hold.

'Forget it, Jason.' Her frigid tone stopped his move to reclaim her. 'I'm going to call my sister and tell her I'm coming home.' She paused, then added pointedly, 'If I may use your phone?'

'It's in the kitchen.' Jason's lip curled in a sneer as his eyes roamed insultingly over her. 'I hope your sisters appreciate what you're sacrificing for them, but I doubt it. Some day they're going to leave you flat . . . then what will you do? Spend the rest of your life making candles?'

Lord, had she actually considered the possibility of a permanent union with this man? Brandy wondered as she stared into his contemptuous face. She had been going out with him on a steady basis for over four months and she didn't even know him, had had no inkling of the disdain he felt for her work. At least the others had evidenced a respect for her craft . . . or had they? Brandy suddenly felt tired beyond belief.

'The phone, Jason.' Her detached, withdrawn tone was designed to reach him, and it did. With a careless shrug he walked away, indicating that she follow him. Inside the small kitchen he disconnected the orange wall phone's receiver and handed it to her with a mocking courtesy.

Brandy took the receiver from him without comment and punched out her home number on the tiny buttons set into the inside of the instrument.

'Hel . . . hello?' Darcy answered on the second ring, her voice sounding strange, hesitant.

'It's Brandy, honey,' Brandy's voice mirrored her frown. 'Are you all right?'

'I am now that Mr Waring's here,' Darcy assured her.

'Mr Waring?' Brandy echoed blankly then, sharply, 'What's he doing there, Darcy?'

'I called him. You see . . .'

'You what?' Brandy interrupted in astonishment. 'Why did you . . . never mind, I'm coming home, and your explanation had better be good!'

All too aware of Jason, unabashedly listening to her end of the exchange, Brandy hung up on her sister.

'Problems, little mother?' Jason taunted from directly behind her.

'Will you take me home?' Brandy asked through clenched teeth. 'Or should I call for a taxi?'

'I'll take you.' Although he did not add 'and good riddance' the phrase was implicit in his tone.

At that moment Brandy was unconcerned with what his tone implied or his face expressed. Other than the fact that he walked beside her to the car, and sat beside her once they were inside it, Jason had little substance for her. During the short drive from his apartment to her home, anxiety filled her to the exclusion of all else.

Her mind ran rampant in speculation about what could have happened to cause Darcy to call Mitchell Waring.

Mitchell Waring, for heaven's sake!

Brandy's hand grasped for the door release when Jason turned the car on to her street, and she swung the door open even as he brought the car to a stop in front of her home.

'Goodnight, Brandy.'

Jason's strained voice arrested her in mid-flight.

With one leg already thrust outside the car, she paused long enough to murmur with quiet finality:

'Goodbye, Jason.'

Then she was moving, the car door slamming behind her, her slim high heels tapping a staccato beat as she hurried across the pavement and up the three shallow steps to the red-painted front door.

Key at the ready, she muttered a soft 'damn' against nervous fingers that made several inefficient jabs at the slot in the lock before making contact. Sighing with relief, she pushed the door inward, completely immune to the angry roar of the sports car as Jason tore away from the curb.

Every sense alert, Brandy drew a deep, steadying breath as she quietly closed the door, then, straightening her shoulders, she hurried up the carpeted stairs. At the entrance way to the living room she came to a dead stop, anxiety and confusion giving way to a hot surge of anger at the scene that met her eyes.

Darcy, dressed for bed in pyjamas and fuzzy robe, sat in the corner of the sofa, her legs drawn up beside her, her face alight with laughter at something the large, relaxed-looking man sitting opposite her had obviously just said.

Mitchell Waring was the first to sense a third presence in the room. His movement casual, he transferred his alert, hazel-eyed gaze from one sister to the other, drawing Darcy's glance with his own.

'Oh, hi, Brandy.'

CHAPTER FOUR

BRANDY'S teeth ground together in fury at the carefree sound of her sister's voice. Here she had spent the last fifteen or twenty minutes imagining all kinds of dire happenings, only to walk in on this scene of laughing relaxation. It was enough to boil the blood of a saint!

'Darcy, I want an explanation, in full, and I want it *now*.' Brandy's voice held a slightly strangled sound, pushed as it was through her teeth.

'Miss Styer——'

Brandy's eyes sliced to Mitchell Waring's with the deadly swiftness of a flashing rapier, her voice slashed across his with a like effect.

'I am speaking to my sister, *sir*,' she grated coldly. '*If* you don't mind?' She didn't wait for an answer. Re-pinning her icy gaze on Darcy's shocked face, she snapped, 'At once, Darcy!'

'Brandy, what are you so mad about?' Darcy's tone held both confusion and astonishment.

'Answer your sister, Darcy.'

Brandy was in no way grateful for Mitchell Waring's unwanted help. She was even less pleased to observe the effect his gentle command had on Darcy.

'I called Mitch because I was frightened.'

'Frightened?' Brandy's eyes scanned the room, as if looking for a visual back-up to Darcy's defence. 'Frightened of what?'

'A phone call.'

'A phone call?' Brandy repeated blankly, then, impatiently, 'Darcy, I——'

'Start at the beginning, kid,' Mitchell Waring interjected smoothly.

Very near the end of her tether now, Brandy kept her eyes on Darcy, while her fingers curled into her palm.

'Karen and Bev went up to bed after the programme they were watching on TV went off at ten o'clock.' Darcy paused to wet her lips and Brandy frowned at the hunted expression that crept into her eyes. 'The programme I always watch from ten till eleven had just gone on when the phone rang.' Here she hesitated, her eyes flickering fearfully at the phone as if it were some sort of instrument of torture. 'When I said hello a man said he was coming right over, and—and then he started saying things.'

'Things?' Brandy prompted, even though by then she knew.

'Things he was going to do to me; sick things. At first I was so shocked I just seemed to freeze, then I hung up. Brandy, I was so scared, I—I kept hearing him saying he was coming right over and—well, I guess I panicked.' Darcy's eyes, cloudy with re-membered fear, sought the reassuring size of her former employer. 'I looked Mitch's number up in the phone book and he told me to sit tight, he'd be right over.'

Brandy felt a stabbing sense of betrayal as she had a flashing image of Darcy, completely ignoring the piece of paper on which she had written down the phone number of the restaurant, frantically paging through the telephone directory for Mitchell Waring's number.

'And here I am,' his smooth voice drew her eyes and attention. 'I had a good look around outside, both front and back—I found nothing unusual. I feel sure it was no more than someone's sick idea of a joke.'

At his words a question jumped into Brandy's mind and she addressed it, as well as her gaze, to Darcy. 'Did you recognise the voice at all?'

Darcy's head was moving negatively before Brandy had finished speaking. 'No, the voice was real low, and kinda rough. It scared me.'

'Well, of course it scared you!' Brandy exclaimed. 'But what I don't understand is why didn't you call *me*, at the restaurant. It wasn't necessary to bother Mr Waring.'

'I was not in the least "bothered", Miss Styer.' A small, mocking smile twisted his firm lips. 'Now, don't you think it's time for all good teenagers to be in bed?'

Brandy picked up on this hint at once. He obviously wanted to discuss this nocturnal phone abuser, but not in front of the caller's victim.

'Yes,' she agreed at once. 'Darcy, you look about to fall asleep on the spot. Go to bed, honey, and don't concern yourself any more about this—I'll take care of it.' Brandy was relieved to note that her tone conveyed a lot more confidence than she was feeling at that moment. Luckily Darcy heard and believed that sound of confidence, for she got to her feet, covering a yawn with her hand.

'Okay, Brand,' she mumbled around her hand, then, more clearly, 'I'm sorry if I upset you.' She made a move to the doorway where she paused to send an adoring smile at her willing protector. 'Thanks, Mitch, you're a teddy-bear!' Darcy left the room in the warmth of Mitchell Waring's bark of amused laughter.

An unwilling captive to the entrancing sound rumbling from his throat, Brandy stared in bemused wonder, seemingly caught in an instant of time

suspension. When, getting to his feet, he turned to
face her, she came down to earth with a thud.

'Is the boy-friend waiting for you?'

The change in him was total—voice, face, the
tautness of his tall frame which, a fleeting moment
ago, had appeared so lazily relaxed.

Brandy had the chilling sensation of being suddenly
submerged in an icy pool of water. Without her
striving for it, her tone reflected that chill.

'I beg your pardon?'

'I asked if your date was waiting for you?' His
needle-sharp eyes swept her now rigidly held body.

'Of course not,' Brandy denied stiffly, oddly shaken
by his insolently dismissive glance. 'It's after eleven-
thirty.' Suddenly remembering Darcy's frightening
phone call, and appalled at herself for forgetting it
even for a moment, she realised the implied insult in
his question. 'You . . . you think I'd go back out, leave
the girls alone after what's happened?' Brandy's voice
shook, as much from hurt as righteous anger.

His shrug was every bit as dismissive as his glance
had been. 'A natural assumption.' Another ripple
moved those massive shoulders, another cold-eyed
perusal raked her encompassingly. 'You haven't
removed your coat, or even put your handbag down.'

'I—I never even thought of it.' The object
mentioned dropped from her hand to land with a soft
plop on to the chair by which she was standing. The
movement of her hand to the top botton on her coat
galvanised him into motion and, moving with an agile
swiftness Brandy would not have believed possible for
a man of his size, he crossed the room to assist her.

His nearness was irrationally unnerving and Brandy,
thinking somewhat wildly that standing next to him
was not unlike standing in the shadow of a looming

mountain, willed her trembling fingers to unfasten the four large buttons on her coat.

'I was upset, and never gave a thought to my coat or bag.' Even as the words tumbled from her lips, she was upbraiding herself for making the excuse. Mitchell Waring held no claim to an explanation from her. So why had she offered one? she grimaced in self-disdain, yet was at the same time thankful he now stood behind her and did not see it.

'I think you were upset over more than Darcy's charming phone call.'

Brandy was electrified, but it was a toss-up over what had shocked her more, his sarcastically drawled assertion, or the fiery sensation the touch of his fingers sent scurrying over her skin when he lifted the garment off her shoulders. The fact that she made no protest when he casually tossed her most treasured article of clothing on top of her handbag was a telling indicator of her shaken composure.

'Wh—what do you mean?' Brandy moved to turn and face him, but was halted by the clamping grip of his long, broad hands on her shoulders. Directing her with pressure from his fingers, he propelled her to the small, ornately framed oval mirror that graced the wall just inside the living room doorway. The mirror was illuminated by two steadily burning candles, set into matching sconces flanking it.

.'Take a good look,' he advised her softly, his eyes meeting hers in the silvered glass. 'Shall I tell you what I see?'

Brandy, disobeying his order, did not look at herself, but instead studied his reflection. What she saw sent a fingertip line of ice down her spine.

His face was frightening in its very stillness, his features seemingly locked into place, causing his cheek and jawbones to jut into hard prominence. His mouth made a slashing line across his face, but it was his eyes that trapped Brandy's gaze and breath. With an intensity that was shattering, his hazel eyes stared into hers, and she could only hope that the glittering flame that leapt in their depths was merely a reflection of the candleglow—and not the fury she feared it was. In her confusion, she never questioned why he should be furious with her.

'Shall I tell you what I see?'

Brandy blinked at the deadly menace in his soft, low tone as he repeated his question, and refocused her gaze to her own countenance.

'I see a woman, a beautiful woman,' he growled close to her ear. 'A beautiful—dishevelled—woman who bears the evidence of a man's passion on her lovely mouth.'

A warning shiver trembled through Brandy's body as her gaze, following the line of his, fastened on the image of her own kiss-swollen, quivering lips. Her warning premonition was proved when, catching her completely off guard, he spun her around to face him.

'Damn him!'

Lost within her strange, never before experienced, fearful reaction to a male, Brandy was barely aware of his muttered imprecation. She was, however, fully aware of that slashing mouth moving closer, closer to her own.

A moment before his lips made contact with hers, his hands slid down her back. His arms enclosed her, drawing her close to his elongated frame, and Brandy had an unreal, dreamlike feeling of being engulfed. Then mouth-to-mouth contact was made and the engulfment was total.

With a silent sigh Brandy parted her lips, allowing

herself to be drawn into the eddying swirl created by his mouth. Mindless, boneless, conscienceless, she wrapped her arms around his strong neck and clung, sweetly drowning in the hot, moist devastation of his kiss.

'Good God, I knew it!'

Brandy was dazedly attempting to puzzle out the meaning of the words he had groaned against her lips when he moved, drawing her full attention to his hands, arching and moulding her into the cradle-like hollow of his leg-parted stance.

Stark awareness of his blatant maleness, of her own trembling femininity splintered through her, tiny shards blazing into the most outer, and inner reaches of her being.

Fast on the heels of awareness came fear of the unknown, followed swiftly by the anger of self-protectiveness. She wanted—no, ached—to abandon all sense of self, identity within the sensuous maelstrom of needs and desire he had so effortlessly submerged her into.

The fury of self-preservation saved her, lending her the strength to tear herself away from what she felt sure would be her own immolation.

'You're out of line, Waring.' Brandy's voice was edged by the rawness of her emotions as she backed away from him warily.

His eyes followed her jerky, backward progress, their colour clouded by a blazing hunger that scared the hell out of her.

'Perhaps, at the beginning.' Amazingly, he agreed with her charge—at first. Then he cancelled that agreement by adding, his own tone raw, 'But only at the beginning. You wanted me, Brandy.'

The flat finality of his statement increased the agitation churning inside her tenfold.

'No!' Brandy shook her head in sharp denial.

'You drank every bit as deeply of the well of desire as I did.' His voice was soft, yet firm with conviction. 'You still want me.'

It was true! Damn him, every word he'd uttered was true. Resentment, of him, of her own newly discovered weakness, put iron into her resolve and steel into her voice.

'All I want is for you to get out of here.'

A small, unnervingly understanding smile lifted the corners of his tight-lipped mouth.

'All right, darling.' The smile spread at her gasp of protest at the endearment. 'I won't push it,' he went on even more softly. 'At least not tonight. But listen carefully, and heed me well: your days of freedom are numbered—my love.'

Wide-eyed with disbelief at what she'd heard, Brandy stared at Mitchell Waring for long, tension-filled seconds, the mocking sound of his last two words echoing with sickening clarity in her mind.

'Get out of my house.' Brandy knew that had her voice not been so hoarse, the command would have been screamed at him. Sheer, unreasoning terror held her in its grip and she had to fight the growing urge to run, hide herself away from this man-mountain—and maybe even herself.

Sending out a silent prayer of thanks, she watched through fear-brightened eyes as he bent and scooped an elegantly tailored topcoat from the back of a chair. Two long-legged strides took him to the doorway where he paused to shoot her an amusement-filled, self-satisfied glance.

'I'll be around,' he promised—threatened?—'often.' Then he was gone, his quiet laughter drifting back from the stairway to torment her.

An hour later Brandy lay wakeful and restless on her suddenly uncomfortable bed, her mind refusing to let go of the scene that had taken place between her and Mitchell Waring.

One question above all others threatened to drive her to the point of distraction. Why, why, why had she responded to him like that? It was not her style. It was not *her*, period. Always before, in all such—physical— encounters, she had kept cool hands on the reins of passion, both hers and whatever man who had been participating. Yet with this man she did not even like, this domineering, arrogantly masculine Mitchell Waring, she had not only let the reins slip, she had flung them aside.

Brandy shuddered at the memory. What in the world kind of madness had possessed her? Had she been rendered vulnerable by not only an evening, but an entire week of unsettling events? Brandy grasped at the idea like a condemned man grasps at the hope of reprieve.

When the phone on the nightstand by her bed rang with startling shrillness in the quiet darkness of her room, Brandy actually jumped.

Could it be the same disgusting caller who had frightened Darcy earlier? Fearfully, her palms suddenly moist, she snatched up the receiver on the second shrill ring.

'Hel——' she swallowed to wet a fear-dried throat, 'hello.'

'Don't be frightened, it's me.' 'Me' was the perpetrator of her wakeful thoughts. At the sound of his voice fear turned to irritation.

'How dare you ring my phone at this time of night?' Brandy demanded furiously. 'What in hell do you want?'

'Besides you?' he taunted. 'Just to remind you to notify the phone company in the morning to report that obscene call.'

Brandy gritted her teeth in annoyance. 'I need no reminding. Do you think I'm an idiot?'

'I think you are one very sexy woman,' he treated her to his demoralising laughter. 'Are you in bed? Alone and missing me, maybe?'

Brandy's teeth made a tiny, grinding noise. 'Have *you* decided to try your hand at obscene calls?'

'No.' His laughter deepened throatily. 'But I have decided to try my hand at having you—and, believe me, when I decide to do something, I do it.'

Brandy hoped fervently that the crashing sound of her receiver making violent contact with its cradle punctured his eardrums.

Morning found Brandy bleary-eyed and fuzzy-minded from lack of sleep. She told herself lethargically to move, yet she lay still ignoring her own dictates. A low groan escaped her lips when a light tap on her door was followed by Bev's bright, sing-song voice.

'Coffee's made and breakfast's started. Better get it shaking, Brandy, if you want to have time to eat before getting ready for church.'

Telling herself she was a young woman, even if she did feel about two hundred, Brandy stumbled out of bed and tottered to the kitchen, damning the intrusive memory of an unnamed man all the way.

'The bride of Frankenstein lives!' Bev exclaimed with devilish glee when Brandy entered the kitchen.

'Or maybe it's the latest punk rock star,' Karen offered consideringly, placing a steaming cup of coffee in front of Brandy as she sank limply on to a chair.

Darcy stared narrow-eyed at her from across the

table. 'You're not hung-over, are you?' Darcy knew that her elder sister never over-indulged, but, worldly-wise at seventeen, she also knew there could always be a first time for anything.

'No, I'm not hung-over,' Brandy assured Darcy wearily. 'I didn't sleep well, or long enough.' She took a tentative sip of the aromatic brew. 'I'll be fine—as soon as my heart starts beating and my blood starts circulating.'

'Here you go,' Karen crooned soothingly, sliding a plate containing two poached eggs and four quarters of buttered toast in front of her. 'A shot of protein will get the old system in gear.'

'One can but hope,' Brandy drawled, reviving swiftly. 'Thanks, hon.'

As could be expected, the breakfast table conversation consisted mainly of Darcy's late-night caller.

Bev was both shaken and outraged.

'What kind of creep does something like that, Brand?'

'Someone with a problem, I suspect.' Brandy lifted her shoulders in a helpless shrug.

'Yeah,' Bev nodded in agreement. 'Someone whose loose change is rattling around between his ears.'

'Very profound,' Karen drawled, raising her eyes ceilingward as if beseeching help. She was quiet a moment, contemplative, then she glanced sharply at Darcy.

'Could it have been a kid?'

Startled, Darcy shook her head confusedly. 'I don't know. The voice was real low, kinda rough, but I guess it could have been—why?'

'Because I know of a couple of girls at school who've had the same kind of calls, and one of the kids said the voice was familiar but she couldn't put a face to it.'

'You mean it could be someone Darcy might know?' Bev exclaimed.

'It's not unheard-of, honey.' Brandy sighed. 'This could be somebody's sick idea of a joke.'

'Some joke!' Bev snorted.

Brandy barely heard Bev. Her own assertion was echoing in her mind, but in the quiet, unruffled tone of the man who had voiced the same assertion the night before. Thus reminded, she took Darcy to task.

'What I fail to understand,' she levelled a stern glance on Darcy, 'is why you had even considered disturbing Mr Waring?' She very nearly choked on the name.

'He wasn't at all disturbed!' Darcy protested. 'And I don't know what made me think of him. Maybe because he'd been on my mind, having got me that job and everything.'

Well, it was a plausible excuse, Brandy conceded. It did not make it any more palatable, but it was *plausible*. Darcy *had* secured the job in the insurance office through his good graces.

'Mitch was here?' Karen yelped. 'And I missed him?'

'Did he say when he'd be coming again?' Bev questioned eagerly.

Brandy observed her sisters in total bewilderment. How had this happened? she wondered confusedly. They barely knew the man, yet the three teenagers seemed to look on him as some sort of hero or something. A hero? Mitchell Waring?

An uncomfortably clear picture of the scene enacted between herself and the man in question flashed into Brandy's mind. Hardly her idea of a hero. So what was his appeal to the younger Styers? A father figure, perhaps?

Not having the answers to any of her own questions, Brandy mentally shrugged them away, and with them the image of one very disturbing, irritating man.

Feeling the need for action, she pushed her chair away from the table. 'I have to report that call to the phone company,' she explained to the three startled faces turned up to her. 'And we'd better get moving if we're to get to church on time. Hop to it, girls!'

After completing her call, Brandy dashed up the stairs to get dressed, her attention centred on the jobs awaiting her on her return from church.

As it was the end of the month and, as she had made a lunch and shopping date with her best friend for tomorrow, she had her Monday shop straightening, plus the shop's financial end-of-month bookwork to do.

By some miracle they were all decked out and ready to leave the house on time.

As they drove home after church in Brandy's belligerently obstreperous compact car, Brandy quizzed her sisters on their plans for the afternoon, hoping against all odds to snare at least one into giving her a hand in the shop. As she had fatalistically surmised, the odds were against her.

After a hurriedly tossed together and equally hurriedly consumed lunch, Darcy, Karen and Bev made tracks of retreat in three different directions.

First Brandy tackled the cleaning and re-stocking of her shop, salving the pricks of her conscience over the slipshod job she did by vowing to give the shop an extra thorough cleaning next Monday.

Then, a cup of freshly brewed coffee in hand, she settled herself at her very old, rather shaky desk and began chewing the eraser on the end of her pencil to shreds—which gave ample proof that her figuring was not going exactly as she had hoped it would.

When, finally, she pushed her chair back and stood up, the daylight was gone, along with her hopes of solvency.

In a word, she was very nearly broke.

Having transferred the action of her teeth from the eraser to her bottom lip, Brandy gnawed away in vexation, staring reproachfully at the open ledger on her desk.

What in the world was she going to do? Unless business picked up—considerably—she could hang on the way she was going for about two months, *if* she was careful.

Thank heaven winter was almost over, she thought wearily, unmindful of the pain her teeth were inflicting on her soft lip. The winter had been harsh all over most of the country, and Pennsylvania had been no exception. Her own heating bills had been staggering, and she had rarely turned the thermostat above sixty-eight degrees. The electric bills were running a close second to the heating bills. Every week it cost her more money at the supermarket; growing girls consumed a lot of food.

Business should get better in the weeks before Easter—at least it always has, she mused. All I have to do is hang on until we no longer need heat in the house. Once the weather warms up—Brandy groaned aloud. Once the weather grew warmer there would be a whole new list of expenses. Bev had grown a full two inches since last summer and would need all new warm weather clothes. Karen's dentist had insisted that unless Brandy wanted to face the prospect of Karen losing her teeth by the time she was in her mid-twenties, her teeth would have to be straightened by bracing.

Last but by no means least was Darcy's up-coming graduation from high school and the attendant costs involved. Brandy knew Darcy would help defray the cost with her own earnings, but, working part-time, her earnings would not be all that great. Then, come September, Darcy would be going on to college. Even with the scholarship Darcy had been granted, and the money Brandy had set aside out of her parents' insurances, it was going to be a squeaker.

In two years Karen would be ready for college, and a year after that Bev——

'Ouch!' Brandy cried aloud as her teeth punctured the delicate skin of her inner lip and drew blood.

What on earth was she going to do for money?

CHAPTER FIVE

BRANDY had no idea how long she stood, staring at the offending ledger, when the sound of activity emanating from the kitchen scattered the numbers that were playing tag in her mind.

From the amount of clatter being created she guessed that all three of her sisters were home—and hungry!

Squaring her shoulders, she flipped the ledger closed and shoved it into her top desk drawer. As much as she disliked the idea she was going to have to discuss finances with them; the discussion would be a first.

To say her sisters were surprised by the news Brandy had to impart to them would be an understatement. The three girls were cast into shocked silence for some seconds, then they erupted volubly, and all at once.

'But how can that be? I thought Daddy's insurance——'

'There must be something we can do!'

'You're not going to lose the shop, are you, Brandy?'

'Hold it! One at a time, please.' Brandy pitched her voice to cut through the babble. They were sitting around the kitchen table, the remains of their makeshift supper cluttering the formica top. Brandy sipped at her steaming coffee before levelling her gaze on Bev.

'As to Daddy's insurance,' she said flatly, 'what was

left after the funeral expenses was divided equally four ways. I used my share to open the shop. Yours,' her glance encompassed Karen and Darcy, 'was put in trust for your college tuition. Daddy also had some investments that give us a small yearly income—but it in no way covers even the basic living expenses.'

Lifting the cup to her lips, she swallowed the rapidly cooling brew before directing her gaze at Karen.

'At this point the only thing we can do is cut our expenses as much as possible. I realise this won't be easy, but it must be done.'

Rising with a natural grace she was not even aware of possessing, Brandy walked to the kitchen counter to refill her cup from the electric percolator sitting there. Turning back to face her subdued sisters, she rested her gaze on Darcy.

'As to the shop,' Brandy sighed, revealing more than she had intended about her worry over her personal pride of achievement, 'I simply don't know. Let's face it, I produce a luxury item. When economic conditions are rough, as they are now, luxury items are the first things to be struck off almost everybody's list. I'm hoping business improves in the weeks before Easter, but if it doesn't,' she shrugged, somewhat hopelessly, 'and even if it does, it will be no more than a stopgap.'

'But you can't give up your shop!' Darcy exclaimed. 'Brandy, you've put so much time and effort, not to mention *all* your talent into it. You can't give it up!'

'Honey, I don't *want* to give it up.' Again she shrugged, hoping she conveyed an unconcern she was far from feeling. 'But if it comes to the crunch, I will.'

'We'll give up our college money before we let you

do that!' Karen declared determinedly, her head swinging from Darcy to Bev for confirmation, which she received in the form of sharp nods of their heads. '*You* left college to take care of us when Mommy and Daddy died, the least we can do——'

'I do appreciate your offer,' Brandy blinked against the sudden hot moisture that threatened to escape the barrier of her lids. 'But even if I were inclined to accept your offer, which I'm not, I couldn't do it.' The smile she bestowed on the three girls held pride of them as well as love for them.

'I couldn't touch that money if I wanted to,' she explained softly. 'The money is yours, and if, for whatever reason, any one of you decided not to go on to college, that money would be turned over to you on your twenty-first birthday.'

'You set the trust up that way, didn't you?' Darcy accused.

'Yes.'

'But didn't you figure that some day you might need it?' Bev demanded, in a very young, worried tone.

'No,' Brandy smiled gently at the fourteen-year-old. 'I couldn't figure on that money, Bev, simply because it was not mine to consider. That money belongs to you, and Karen and Darcy—for your futures.'

'But what about you?' Karen protested.

'What about me?' Brandy countered. 'I told you, I had my share.'

'Which you used to open a business to help support us,' Darcy joined the fray. 'Brandy, not only did you leave school, but you've given up a life of your own just to take care of us. Now you tell us we can't even help you when you need it.'

'Good lord! I never realised I was so wonderful.' Brandy's grin lightened the tension that had gripped her sisters. 'I've given up nothing of any *real* importance.' The assurance in her tone was easy and unforced, simply because Brandy had never felt any sense of deprivation by caring for her siblings.

'Look, kids, our backs aren't quite to the wall as yet. I just wanted to put you into the picture. We're going to have to budget, stringently. Now,' she stepped briskly away from the countertop, 'let's get this kitchen cleaned up, okay?'

'But——'

Brandy was not to know what objection Bev was going to make, for at that moment a firm rap was lodged against the kitchen door.

'That's probably Ellen,' Karen declared, heading for the door. 'She said she'd come over after supper. We're going to study for a history test tomorrow.'

In the act of squirting detergent into the sink, Brandy stiffened at Karen's happily astonished outcry on opening the door.

'Hey, Mitch, how are ya? Come on in.'

'I'm fine, thank you.' His amused drawl grated on Brandy's nerves, and she clenched her teeth in annoyance as he added: 'And how are you beautiful young ladies today?'

'In the pits,' Bev answered him in honest innocence. Sharp alarm fractured the stillness holding Brandy and she swung around to silence Bev. She was an instant too late.

'What's the problem?' Mitchell Waring enquired as he shrugged out of an elegant suede jacket. He was wearing two pieces of a three-piece suit, navy blue slacks and waistcoat, which along with a pale blue shirt and grey tie gave him a somewhat less formal appearance than he had had on the other two occasions he had been at the house.

'We're poor,' Bev overstated the situation just as Brandy issued a warning, 'Bev!'

'Poor?' Hazel eyes sliced to pin Brandy to the sink, the amusement giving way to hard contemplation. 'Explain.'

Swift anger, combined with an intense memory of the minutes spent in his arms, and of his words the night before, sent a flush to tinge Brandy's cheeks. Explain? The arrogance of his one-word command incensed her. Explain indeed!

'I have no intention of boring you with a recitation of our finances——' she began dismissively, only to be cut off by his abrupt order to her sisters.

'Get lost, girls.' His hard, white teeth flashed in a grin. 'Brandy and I want to fight!'

Giggles of delight met his bland assertion. Fuming, Brandy bit her tongue to hold back a scathing retort until the silly teenagers had disappeared up the back stairs.

'Really, Mr Waring——' Once again she found herself unable to finish speaking.

'Really, my foot!' he snorted. 'What did Bev mean by "poor"?'

'Like most fourteen-year-olds, Bev exaggerates.' Even as she issued the disclaimer, Brandy was wondering how he had managed to become on such easy terms with her sisters. What was it about him that drew their interest and affections? Again the term 'father figure' skipped through her mind. With a sharp shake of her head to dispel her bemusement at the very idea that the girls might need a father figure, Brandy went on the attack.

'Not that it's any of your business, but, along with just about everyone else, things are a little tight right now. We are not—repeat—not poor.' In an attempt to drive home her message of 'butt out', Brandy dipped her tongue in acid. 'Please *do not* concern yourself!'

The narrowing of his eyes left little doubt that her sarcastic message had been received loud and clear. The half smile that touched his lips as he moved slowly towards her left no doubt at all of his intention to disregard her message.

'Why do you bait me, I wonder?'

Brandy gulped spasmodically at the soft menace in his tone. Steeling herself against shrinking back when his towering form came to a stop before her, she threw back her head and glared up at him.

'I do not bait you,' she denied fiercely. 'I do not do anything to you at all.'

Bad choice of words. Brandy knew it even before his soft laughter preceded his equally soft taunt,

'Oh, my intoxicating Brandy, you do *all* kinds of things to me.'

A trembling began in the centre of her body and radiated in rays of heat to her outer covering of skin. This close he loomed enormous and triggered a remembrance of how it had felt to be engulfed within his powerful arms.

How very easy it would be to lose all sense of self in that strong haven. How tempting to shrug off, if just for a moment, the mantle of responsibility and care and worry she had so willingly assumed.

A longing ache invaded her limbs and she actually raised her arms to circle his waist when the realisation of what she was doing splintered through her mind, alerting her to her own weakness.

Was she mad? She didn't even like this man. He was too arrogant, too domineering, much, much too sure of himself. Added to these flaws in his character was the worrying notion that he was trying to usurp her authority, unbelievable as that notion might seem.

The urgent need to defend shot iron into her spine, and blinking away the bemusement his nearness caused, Brandy stared up at him with cold defiance.

'On such short acquaintance,' she essayed frostily, 'I find it hard to believe I have any impact at all on you.'

'It took you *that* long to form that opinion?' He tilted his head slightly to one side, one eyebrow arching mockingly. 'An erroneous opinion, I might add. But we digress,' he went on with sudden, confusing briskness. 'A deliberate ploy to lead me off the point, I think. It didn't work, Brandy. The word "poor" reverberates inside my mind. Either you tell me what Bev meant or I'll go and quiz the girls.'

'I don't use ploys,' Brandy snapped. 'And, as I think I said before, my financial situation is none of your business.'

'I'm making it my business,' he snapped back. 'Damn it, Brandy, don't be so stiffnecked! I'm offering you a loan, if that's what you need.'

'You're not satisfied with playing at the role of protector?' she chided over-sweetly, still stung by the fact that Darcy had thought of him first the night before. 'You now want to play the role of banker as well?'

The force with which he grasped her shoulders startled a soft 'oh!' from her lips. The light shake he administered silenced the spate of protest that rose in her throat.

'Yes, you exasperating woman, I want to play banker.' He glared down at her, the brown flecks in his hazel eyes taking on a golden sheen in his anger. 'I want to play the role of protector and banker, father and brother, friend and confidante, but,' his gaze bored into her, 'most important of all, I want the coveted role of *lover*.'

Lover. Lover. Lover. The word ricocheted inside Brandy's mind and in an attempt to dislodge it she shook her head dazedly.

'Are——' she had to pause to wet lips that felt like parchment to the tip of her tongue. 'Are you out of your——'

His mouth silenced her. His kiss was not designed to be tender. Punishing, subjecting, demoralising, yes—but in no way tender.

Caught, as she had been, with her lips parted, Brandy was wide open to the devastating effect of his demanding mouth. She should have turned to stone with rejection, but contrarily she turned to mush with response.

The low groan that tore from the back of her throat, whether caused by his convulsively gripping fingers or the riot of sensations coursing through her, flowed into his mouth and, as the whispery sound filled his head, he wrenched his mouth from hers.

'Yes, I'm out of my mind.' His low growl answered the question she had begun what now seemed ages ago. 'I'm out of my mind with wanting you. Let me help you, darling.'

The endearment washed over her with the force of an arctic wave. Beginning to struggle in his now painful grip, Brandy, fearing the passion that shook his tall frame, lashed out wildly.

'You want? *You* want? I don't *care* what you want. *I* don't want *you* or your help, Mr Waring!'

'Damn your stubborn independence,' he grated through his teeth. 'Do you think I'm a fool? I felt your response to me, both last night and just now.' His fingers dug even more deeply into her soft flesh.

'You're hurting me, Mr Waring.' Although she strove to keep her tone cool, the tremor on its edge proclaimed her failure.

'I'll do more than hurt you if you call me Mr Waring one more time,' he warned. His fingers punished her ruthlessly. 'I want to hear my name on your lips.' He paused for half a second. '*Now*, Brandy.'

'M-Mitchell.' Brandy hated herself for obeying, yet obey she did.

'I prefer Mitch, but I'll settle for Mitchell.'

Brandy could not deny the sigh of relief that escaped as his hold on her loosened. For a few moments there he had frightened her, really frightened her, and her expressive sigh revealed her fear to him.

'You know, I've never before felt the need to inflict pain on a woman.' Mitch's tone held wonder, and a touch of self-condemnation. 'You anger me beyond reason, and excite me beyond endurance.' Lowering his head, he brushed her gasp of shock away with his warm lips. 'I'm going to have to do something about you very soon, my Brandy, or take the risk of going over the edge of reason *and* endurance.' Once more his lips brushed hers, slowly, lingeringly. 'Let me help you.'

Bemused by the tingling of her kiss-swollen lips, the renewed hammering of her pulses, Brandy stared up at him, her grey eyes cloudy with indecision. Inside her a war was being waged between her common sense and her physical senses. She *knew* she should push him away, tell him to get out of her house and never come back. Some sixth sense was shouting a warning that if she did not send him away now, she would be in danger of being engulfed by him.

She heard the warning, yet she also heard the

pleading of her physical senses that begged to be appeased, even at the cost of total capitulation.

As if he was fully aware of her silent, inner battle, Mitch held her eyes in a visual vice, his intent gaze promising a glimpse of heaven if she would only give in.

Had he kissed her then, at that moment, she would have been lost. He did not, and the moment was gone, shattered by a light tapping on the kitchen door.

Blinking her eyes as if coming out of a trance, Brandy brought her trembling hands to his broad, flatly muscled chest and pushed, thankful that from where they stood at the sink, they could not be seen through the window in the back door. Her puny effort at moving him was as effective as a small snow-plough trying to dislodge an iceberg.

'Mitchell, please,' Brandy's tone held the realisation of her near miss. 'There's someone at the door.'

The grimace that twisted his lips gave proof of his own realisation that he had, by allowing her time to fight her inner battle, blown his chances for now. A fatalistic shrug rippling the width of his shoulders, he stepped back.

'Don't let this minor victory go to your head,' he advised in a dangerously soft tone. 'Ready or not, like it or not, your independent days are numbered, Brandy.' Turning with casual ease, he strolled to the bottom of the back stairs, pausing long enough to deliver a parting shot. 'When I want something badly enough, I always get it, and I want you very, very badly.'

Before Brandy could even open her mouth to retort he disappeared up the stairwell.

'Arrogant bastard!'

Brandy wasn't even aware that she'd muttered the

indictment aloud as she turned the lock and opened
the door. Karen's friend Ellen stood on the back step,
her face a study in confusion.

'Were you talking to me, Brandy? I didn't hear what
you said.'

Thank heaven! Forcing a semblance of a smile to
her stiff-with-anger lips, Brandy shook her head in
denial.

'No, Ellen, I was talking to myself.' Stepping back,
she allowed the girl entrance, all the while wondering
if Mitch was busily pumping her sisters. 'A sign of
premature ageing, do you suppose?'

'I hope not,' the pretty teenager laughed. 'I do it all
the time.'

Not using quite the same language, I hope. The
thought brought a shadow of genuine amusement to
Brandy's stiff smile. Telling the girl to go on up to the
living room, she set to clearing the still cluttered table.

Her movements automatic from much experience,
Brandy was free to ponder her own recent con-
tradictory emotions.

What in the green, sweet world had come over her?
Never, but never had she reacted like that to a man,
and the fact that it was this particular man baffled her
all the more. She had felt an antipathy to him on sight.
Come to think of it, *that* had never happened to her
before either.

Totally unaware that she was vigorously wiping the
table for the third time, she went still with
apprehension at the clattering of footsteps on the
stairs. Gearing herself for another confrontation, she
felt oddly deflated when Bev and Darcy preceded
Mitch into the room from the confines of the closed
staircase.   •

'Guess what, Brandy?' All trace of Bev's earlier

dejection was gone. 'Mitch is going to see if he can find me a babysitting job too,' she bubbled. 'Then *I'll* be able to do my part in helping out with the money.'

Too? Her mind caught on that one word, Brandy barely assimilated Bev's last, proudly delivered statement.

'Too?' she repeated aloud, her glance shifting to the large presence she had deliberately been avoiding.

'One of the reasons I stopped by this evening,' Mitch obliged smoothly, 'was to ask Karen if she'd be interested in sitting for friends of mine.'

'I see.' The sensation of having the reins of control torn out of her hands crept over Brandy, threatening the measure of composure she had managed to achieve. Telling herself she was being fanciful, she forced a degree of cool interest into her tone. 'What has that to do with Bev?'

'She asked if I might know of anyone else in need of a sitter, and I——'

'And he said he might!' Bev's excited exclamation rudely interrupted his explanation. 'He said he knew of one woman in particular who would be needing someone soon, as the sitter she has now is pregnant and won't be able to work much longer.'

Her gaze having skipped to Bev's animated face, Brandy again shifted her glance in question.

'Actually, the woman works for me, and what she needs is more in the way of a mother's help,' Mitch smiled easily. 'The young woman she has now keeps the house straightened and gets supper for the children on Thursday and Friday as well as being there all day Saturday. Consequently, as she expects more, she pays more.'

'Thursday and Friday?' Beginning to feel as if her

head was on a swivel, Brandy looked back to Bev. 'What time Thursday and Friday?'

'From right after school,' Bev replied gleefully.

'But you can't do that!' Brandy, her composure disintegrating, exclaimed sharply. 'What about all your school activities? The school show?'

'I'll drop out.' Although Bev tried a careless shrug, she was unsuccessful in masking the disappointment momentarily revealed in her expression. 'Earning money is more important now.'

'No!' Brandy's voice was shrill with anger. This was absolutely more than she could tolerate! This—this man-mountain had finally pushed too hard. When her glance swept back to him this time her grey eyes were stormy. 'Damn you and your interference! I *will not* allow Bev to give up her school activities for a few dollars a week!' Before the surprised man she was glaring at could reply, she spun back to her sister. 'Bev, you may *not* take a job if it interferes with your extra-curricular activities. You've talked about this school show for weeks, so don't try convincing me it means nothing to you.'

'But, Brandy, I want to help,' Bev wailed. 'And if Mitch can get me——'

'Now, wait a min——' Mitch began interrupting Bev, only to be interrupted himself by a now thoroughly irate Brandy.

'No, you wait, *Mr* Waring!' Not even bothering to look at him, Brandy, her hands firmly planted on her hips, proceeded to take Bev to task. 'We are not about to starve. If I gave you the impression earlier that we were, I'm sorry. If you really want to help me, you can do so by getting a well rounded education. This mother's help job *Mr* Waring has mentioned is out of the question.'

The sight of Bev's quivering lower lip, the brightness of her eyes, caused a tightness in Brandy's throat. Walking to the girl, she drew her gently into her arms.

'Honey,' she murmured, 'you'll never know how proud I am of you right now—how proud I am of all three of my sisters. Please believe me, you don't have to get a job.'

'But I want to help,' Bev sniffed.

'I know you do,' Brandy soothed. 'And you can.'

'How?' Bev's voice brightened perceptibly.

'You could take over some of Darcy's and Karen's chores here at home,' Brandy suggested. 'They may even be willing to pay you.'

'I know I would,' Darcy, speaking for the first time since coming downstairs, agreed with fervour. Unlike Bev, who enjoyed doing housework, Darcy hated the daily chores, much preferring the stimulation of an outside job. 'C'mon, Bev, let's go see what Karen thinks of the idea.'

'Okay.' With a quicksilver change of mood, Bev gave Brandy a fierce hug, then turned to follow Darcy up the stairs. Her foot on the bottom tread, she paused to smile endearingly at Mitch. 'Thanks anyway, Mitch.'

'You bet, kid!' Mitch returned her smile with his lips. Only Brandy noticed that the smile didn't reach his eyes.

Put on guard by his smile that was not a smile at all, she lifted her chin and stared directly into his frost glazed eyes.

'I'd like you to leave now.' Brandy's tone was every bit as cold as his eyes. 'I think you've caused enough havoc for one night, don't you?'

'Dammit, Brandy, I had no idea the kid was so

involved in school. If I'd known, I wouldn't have suggested the job for her.' Much to Brandy's surprise, a ruddy tinge brushed his cheeks. 'I, too, only wanted to help.'

'You don't want to help,' Brandy denied scathingly. 'For some unfathomable reason of your own, you want to take over. Well, I'm not going to let you. I want you to go.'

The ruddy hue was gone from his suddenly harshly etched face, and his eyes fairly snapped sparks at her.

'The girls told me exactly how tight things were getting for you.' His tone betrayed impatience. 'How long can you hold on? Two months? Three? And, if business doesn't pick up, what do you do then?'

'I'll worry about that.'

'But, dammit, you don't have to worry about it. Let me help you.'

'No.' Brandy stared defiantly at him. 'Now, will you please go?'

'You're an exasperating, stubborn——' Mitch cut himself off in mid-tirade. 'I've grown rather fond of the girls,' he drawled sarcastically. 'I hope you don't mind if I drop by occassionally to see them?'

'Be my guest.' Brandy matched him for sarcasm.

'Oh, I will, my sweet,' he promised with shivering softness. 'I most definitely will!'

CHAPTER SIX

'I MOST definitely will.'

The words seemed to come out of the mouth of the newscaster, and with a sigh Brandy got up and switched off the TV ten minutes into the local news programme.

In those minutes she had absorbed nothing of the commentator's report as Mitchell Waring's warning rang incessantly in her mind, as indeed it had ever since he had taken his leave, after one last wicked parting smile.

Now, hours later, Brandy was still fighting the nervous agitation that his promise, backed up by his smile, had created throughout her entire being.

Why was it, she wondered, that this one particular man had the power to rattle her so? Mitchell Waring was, without question, *the* most over-confident, overbearing, arrogant man she had ever had the misfortune to meet. He could set her teeth on edge without halfway trying. Because he was the way he was, she had dismissed him from her home. Why could she not dismiss him from her thoughts?

Beginning to feel slightly dizzy from her circling thoughts, Brandy gave up and went to her room. She had slept badly the night before, and at the rate her mind was churning, she was afraid she would fare little better tonight.

Consigning Mitchell Waring to an extremely hot region, she prepared for bed, her concentration centred doggedly on how pleasant it would be to see her friend Missi in the morning.

Should she confide her money worries to Missi? she mused as she slid between cool, welcoming sheets. Missi Ohlinger had known her share of financial rough spots.

Yawning delicately, Brandy snuggled into a comfortable position while conjuring up an image of her best friend.

Small, dark-haired, and vivacious, Missi had faced adversity many times and emerged victorious. The admiration and respect Brandy felt for the tiny bundle of energy who was her dearest friend was enormous and ongoing.

In the first place, Missi's birth had been premature, and simply staying alive had been a struggle. Though no one would know it to look at her now, she had been an anaemic child and had been plagued by throat and chest infections during her formative years.

Brandy had first come to know Missi when they were both assigned to the same second grade classroom. At that time Missi was a small, thin, very pale child with big brown eyes that even then glowed with her intense desire to enjoy everything life had to offer.

They had become friends on the very first day of school, but it was not until they were in their freshman year at Kutztown State Teachers College that Brandy learned that Missi's doctor had not expected her to live more than a few hours. Or that there had been numerous times over the years that life, for Missi, had been a touch-and-go thing.

Luckily, Missi had been blessed with loving, caring parents who had striven to give her as normal a childhood as possible. By the time she was in high school she had outgrown the physical weakness, but years of medical expenses had sadly depleted her parents' finances. Finally healthy, emotionally secure, Missi had happily gone to work at sixteen to help out. She had continued to work part-time during the school months, full-time during vacation periods, ever since.

Now, at twenty-six, Missi was beginning to know a measure of financial freedom. An art major in college, she worked in a small gallery full-time and on her own paintings part-time. That her own work was becoming accepted was proved by the fact that her paintings of the Pennsylvania countryside had given her a larger income the previous year than her job at the gallery.

Although they had remained close friends, they had seen less and less of each other as work and family responsibilities consumed their time. Subsequently, Brandy had been delighted when Missi called to invite her to lunch and an afternoon of shopping.

'The gallery will be closed next Monday,' Missi had told her after their initial greetings. 'The roof sprang a leak and ruined the ceiling plaster and it's being repaired on Monday. And so,' she had added, 'I thought it would be a good time for us to get together and catch up on each other's lives.'

Brandy had agreed at once, and now, drifting very close to sleep, she smiled in anticipation of being with her irrepressible friend again.

Monday dawned bright and mild, a perfect day for leisurely shopping. Eager to see her friend again, Brandy was ready and waiting when Missi pulled up in her used VW rabbit at exactly eleven-thirty. The interior of the small car was filled with laughter and a steady stream of chatter from the moment Brandy slid into the front passenger seat.

It was not until they neared the centre of town that Brandy paused to wonder if Missi had a definite

destination in mind. Speculation ceased and a small
smile curved her lips when Missi drove the small car
into the Prince Street Parking Garage.

'Okay?' Missi asked as she pulled on the handbrake.

'Of course,' Brandy grinned at her friend's self-
satisfied expression.

As they left the parking garage, she fell into step
beside Missi without prompting, now knowing their
destination was a small shop in a row of equally small
buildings. A green awning over the shop's entrance
proclaimed: The Orange Street Tea Shop.

'Good morning, ladies.'

The greeting was enthusiastic and familiar, as was
the smile of welcome on the proprietor's face.

'Are we too early for lunch?' Missi asked, after they
had returned his greeting.

'Not at all,' he beamed, indicating a doorway at the
rear of the narrow shop. 'Go right down.'

As they traversed the length of the shop, Brandy's
eyes darted around the fully stocked shelves. To the
right, both in front and behind the intelligent and, as
Brandy knew, knowledgeable store-keeper, was an
enticing array of exotic teas and coffees. The shelves
on her left were fairly bursting with teapots and
services, and all manner of coffee makers and
accessories.

As always, Brandy had the sensation of stepping
back in time as she descended the enclosed stairway to
the basement dining area, which comprised two small
rooms.

Without consultation, Brandy and Missi moved in
unison to the back room, and mounted the one step up
into an alcove that contained a table for two. The plain
wooden table was double-clothed with a small,
patterned square over the top of a large white cloth.

'Good morning, ladies.' The tall, good-looking young waiter's greeting echoed the one they had received on the floor above. 'Are you having a late morning coffee break or an early lunch?'

'Lunch.' Missi, never able to resist an attractive male face, smiled brilliantly as she swept her gaze over his well-put-together, tall frame.

He loved it. Brandy laughed softly as his smile changed from polite congeniality to distinct interest. After all these years she was well used to the effect her vivacious friend had on the opposite sex.

'Have you seen the bill of fare?' His eyes danced with amusement.

'Not necessary—at least, not for me.' Missi's eyes reflected the light from his. 'Brandy?'

'Me either,' Brandy swallowed her laughter. 'I'll have the quiche and wild strawberry tea.'

'And I'll have the same.' Missi's naturally long eyelashes fluttered almost imperceptibly.

He loved that too.

'At once,' he promised, laughing softly as he turned away.

'Miss Ohlinger, you're an incurable flirt!' Brandy chided her friend teasingly.

'I know,' Missi grinned. 'And boy, it's fun! You should try it some time.'

'I don't have time,' Brandy laughed, then grimaced ruefully. 'Besides, I think I've forgotten how.'

The quiche, as always, was delicious, the aromatic tea soothing. While they ate, they talked non-stop, blithely interrupting each other at regular intervals.

'Okay, Brandy, we've covered just about every minute of our lives since we last talked on the phone.' Missi's change of tone indicated her sudden seriousness. 'Now, do you want to tell me what's bothering you?'

'Bothering me—what do you mean?' Brandy countered, still undecided about confiding her money worries.

'Oh, come on, Brand,' Missi frowned reproachfully. With slow deliberation she let her gaze rest on Brandy's hand. 'You've been tapping your nail against that cup handle for five minutes. What's eating at you? The kids giving you problems?'

'No.' Brandy shook her head in denial. 'At least, none I can't cope with.' Lifting her cup, she took a sip of her tea before boldly blurting, 'I'm almost broke, Missi, and I haven't the vaguest idea what to do about it.'

'The economic crunch, hmm?'

'Yes.'

'I know.' Missi smiled her understanding. 'Business is off at the gallery too.'

'The thing is,' Brandy sighed, 'even if business picks up, finances are going to be tight, with Darcy going to college in September. I *could* take a mortgage on the house, but I shudder to even think of it.'

'What you need, my friend, is a husband,' Missi declared firmly.

'A what?' Brandy exclaimed.

'Preferably one with a higher than average income,' Missi went on blandly. 'Which reminds me, how is your affair progressing with Jason? Hasn't he popped the all-important question yet?'

'Missi, you're outrageous!' Brandy half laughed, half groaned. 'In the first place, there never was an *affair*.' She actually scowled at her friend.

'Why not? Aren't you as normal as the rest of us?'

'Yes, of course I am—but——'

'But what?'

'I have enough with the girls and the shop,'

Brandy's tone held an edge of exasperation. 'The last thing I need is a physical involvement.'

'Oh, I don't know.' Missi waved her small hand airily. 'You'd probably be a lot less tense.'

'Oh, Missi!' Brandy sighed.

'Well, you would,' her irrepressible friend insisted. 'But you said—in the first place. Is there a second place?'

'Isn't there always?' Brandy shrugged. 'I must have a positive talent for choosing the wrong men. Running true to form, Jason wasn't interested in marriage. He had more of a *relationship* in mind.' Her sigh was deeper this time. 'I suppose I can't blame him, really. What young man would want to take on a ready-made family of teenagers?'

An image of a very tall, very domineering man rose to torment her mind, and with a sharp shake of her head Brandy rejected it.

'Did you say Jason *was*?' Missi probed.

'Yes, was.' Brandy smiled without humour. 'When *I* made it clear I wasn't interested in playing games, *he* made it clear he was no longer interested—period.'

'And there's no one else on the horizon?'

Oh, yes, Brandy thought cynically, there's a very large someone. *He* wants to give me a loan—taking my body as collateral.

'No.' Brandy shook her head, then, in an obvious attempt to change the topic, chided, 'I thought we were going shopping.'

'Okay,' Missi laughed, pushing back her chair, 'I can take a hint!'

As they left the Tea Shop and began strolling up Orange Street towards the Place Marie mini-mall, a large white delivery van, with smart bright red lettering on the side, passed them. Brandy fought back

a grimace as she eyed the blatant red paint that spelled
out—Waring Shops—in elegant script.

'There is one place I definitely want to shop at
today,' Missi nodded at the passing van. 'I saw a pair
of sandals in there last week, and although they're
frightfully expensive, I've decided to give them to
myself as a reward for finishing my last commissioned
painting ahead of schedule.'

'Sheer indulgence,' Brandy teased, swallowing a
groan of dismay; the last store in the world she wanted
to visit today was Waring's.

Nonetheless, little more than an hour later, she
found herself outside the original downtown shop
started by the elder Warings, and now managed by
their only son, Mitchell. Along with everyone else in
the area, she was well aware that there were now four
other shops, laid out exactly like the original one,
scattered throughout south-eastern Pennsylvania.

The shops were unique in that they catered to both
men and women and could provide any and everything
worn on the body from the skin out, inclusive of
cosmetics and scents.

The deep, wide showcase windows were dressed for
spring and beckoned susceptible males and females
with a dazzling display of lightweight, light-coloured
finery. Walking along the recess to the store's heavy
glass entrance doors, Brandy was hard put to it to
smother a sigh of longing over the latest in warm
weather fashions, artfully arranged in the window to
her left.

Inside, the large store was laid out to coincide with
the display windows; ladies' apparel to the left,
menswear to the right, continuing to the shoe
department at the rear of the store. A series of elegant
glass showcase islands made a staggered line through

the centre of the huge room, separating the sexes, so to speak. It had been at one of these islands that Darcy had suffered her momentary fall from grace. Unable to prevent herself from doing so, she looked away from the fine line of cosmetics as she walked by that particular island.

Like a homing pigeon, Missi made a beeline to the shoe department.

'If I even pause to look,' she admitted in a whisper, 'I'll wind up buying a complete outfit to go with the sandals, so I'm not even going to peek at the clothes as I go by!'

Brandy went Missi one further, *she* didn't even look at the shoes. She admired the sandals Missi was captured by, then, as Missi went to the counter to pay for her purchase, found her own gaze caught by a champagne beige handbag in marshmallow leather. Giving in to the desire to touch, she strolled to the handbag showcase to examine the bag more closely. Her fingers were on the clasp when all thought was sent flying out of her mind.

'Hello, Brandy.'

A whisper. A greeting. A caress. The two words were all three and more, and Brandy felt the effect all the way to the pit of her stomach. Unaware that her nails were digging into the supple leather, she raised her eyes slowly to the source of the nerve-tingling sound. As grey eyes met hazel, Mitchell Waring smiled in sweet beguilement.

Ah, gee!

The concise, if inelegant, phrase filled the space of her suddenly empty mind. Ah, gee, why did he have to look so good? Without a flicker of movement her gaze encompassed the look of him in a dark suit, pale blue shirt—it *would* be silk—and patterned tie.

Obviously experiencing none of the reticence that afflicted her, his eyes travelled at a bold, leisurely pace from her breeze-tousled short curls to her black high-heeled slingbacks.

The width of the leather goods counter separated them yet, by the time his eyes came back to her, Brandy felt as if every burning inch of her body had known the touch of his broad, long-fingered hands.

It was a devastatingly exciting feeling. Too devastatingly exciting. Shock at her own reaction jarred her mind into activity and her tongue into speech.

'Hello, Mitchell.'

The smile that played over his beautiful male lips reinforced the warmth rising to tinge her cheeks. Had he been aware of the time lapse between his greeting and her response? Dumb question, Brandy, she chided herself; this man was aware of everything.

'I—I——' Brandy could have bitten her tongue in punishment for refusing to work properly. What was wrong with her, anyway? She was stammering like an embarrassed teenager, and she had never done that when she *was* a teenager!

'Yes?' he prompted gently.

'I—just hadn't expected to see you here, I suppose.' Oh, that was brilliant, Brandy, she derided her own inanity. Why would you not expect to see him in one of his stores? Mitchell was quick to confirm her own self-derision.

'I don't see why not, I work here.'

His more than merely attractive face was a picture of seriousness, yet he was laughing at her. Damn his overgrown hide! He was laughing at *her*! The realisation was all that was needed to smooth the knots from her tongue.

'Yes, I know.' Brandy was rather proud of the

sweetly condescending tone she'd achieved.
Satisfaction shivered through her as she saw a wary
expression cross his face as she continued, 'But then
you have so *many* stores to choose from to work in.
Surely one might even be forgiven for the assumption
that, perhaps, the oh-so-rich Mitchell Waring may
choose not to work at all.'

Watching his lids narrow over the flame of
annoyance that leapt into his eyes, Brandy felt a thrill
of exhilaration pierce her. Yes indeed, baiting the
man-mountain was decidedly enjoyable.

'It bothers you?'

Brandy blinked in confusion. His tone had been
blandly smooth. Darn it, he wasn't annoyed at all!

'I beg your pardon?'

'You should.' Mitchell's eyes now held a sheen of
amusement. 'Resenting someone else's material wealth
is not your style, so *I* must assume I've been singled
out for that honour.' A grin of pure delight revealed
his strong white teeth. 'I wonder why?'

Goodnight, nurse, what was he implying? Brandy
knew, of course, but she stubbornly refused to face it.

'I haven't the vaguest idea what you're talking
about.' Unnerved, she looked away restlessly. What
was taking Missi so long?

'Oh, I think you do,' Mitchell's assertion drew her
unwilling gaze back to his. 'But this is hardly the place
to discuss it. Were you looking for someone?'

'Yes—my friend.' Brandy's eyes scanned the area
again, a small smile curving her lips as she caught
sight of Missi, laughing up at the young salesman as
he handed her her bagged purchase. As she turned
away from the young man, Missi's eyes widened at
sight of Mitchell.

'Hi, Mitch!' As she walked up to them, Missi's

glance, alive with curiosity, darted from Mitch to Brandy and back again to the tall man. 'I had no idea you two knew each other.'

'We—er—met recently.' Mitchell's hesitation was barely perceptible, yet Missi's brows arched questioningly. 'Through young Darcy,' he answered her silent query, then, forestalling further questions, asked, 'How are you, Missi?'

The ensuing spate of conversation was lost on Brandy as her mind replayed the circumstances by which she had come to meet the large, intimidating Mitchell Waring.

'Excuse me, Mitch.'

Brandy's wandering attention was captured by the husky, unfamiliar new voice. Glancing up from the handbag she had been unseeingly staring at, her gaze encountered a tall, voluptuous, honey-blonde woman who was not quite a raving beauty, but very close to it.

'Yes, Donna?' For some obscure reason, the smile that Mitchell gave the woman caused an odd, quirky pain in Brandy's chest.

'I'm sorry to interrupt, but there's a call for you from New York.' The husky-voiced Donna returned his smile, and the quirky pain delved deeper into Brandy's chest. 'It's about that overdue shipment you've been ranting about,'—her smile grew—'or I would have taken it myself.'

'Right,' Mitchell's smile went cold. 'I want to take that call. Go and keep them on the line, I'll be with you in a moment.'

Brandy did not see the woman walk away as she was once again staring sightlessly at the beige bag, unaware that her fingers caressed the supple leather.

'If you're interested in the bag, I'll call a clerk over.' Mitchell's impatient tone drew her startled glance.

'No,' Brandy shook her head. Dammit, he *knew* her financial situation! 'You know I can't——' she broke off, catching the gleam of interest in Missi's expression. 'Not today. Your caller is waiting.'

'He'll wait,' he stated confidently.

Brandy ground her teeth against an irritated retort. Even so, her tone held an edge.

'How nice for you,' Brandy's smile narrowed his lids. 'But business before pleasure—however dubious.'

'I assure you there was nothing dubious about the pleasure of seeing you—both of you—again.' That was what his mouth said. His eyes said: You're in trouble, girl.

Brandy repressed a shudder as she watched his retreating form stride towards a stairway at the very back of the store after he had murmured a coolly polite, 'Good afternoon.'

Missi was suspiciously quiet as they retraced their path out of the store. The minute they were back on the sidewalk she erupted like a mini volcano.

'What the devil was that all about?' she demanded, wide-eyed with curiosity.

'Nothing, really.' Brandy gave a fair imitation of a careless shrug. 'Mr Waring and I don't get on too well.'

'I'll say!' Missi laughed. 'I could almost see the sparks flying! Too bad,' she swept Brandy with a calculating look. 'He'd be perfect for the role I mentioned earlier.'

'What do you mean?' Brandy asked blankly, knowing full well what Missi meant.

'The role of husband, of course.'

'Missi, honestly!' Brandy exclaimed.

'But it would be perfect,' Missi sighed. 'Besides being oh-so-very tall and handsome, he has all those stores, and all that money. What more could a girl ask for?'

'Compatibility,' Brandy snapped repressively.

'I guess it's just as well,' Missi grinned. 'the way I hear it, the gorgeous Amazon holds pride of place—has for some time now.'

Brandy ignored the renewal of the quirky pain. 'You mean the woman who came to tell him about the call?' she asked, playing dumb.

'The same.'

'Are they engaged or something?'

'Or something.' Missi laughed. 'She's married.'

'Married?' Brandy repeated faintly. Somehow she could not picture Mitchell Waring in the role of poacher.

'With two kids.' Missi paused at Brandy's disbelieving expression. 'Two,' she repeated flatly. 'They call him Uncle Mitch,' she drawled dryly.

Brandy felt suddeny sick. She could actually feel the colour deserting her face, and in an effort to hide her reaction, she forced a droll tone and attitude. 'How very sophisticated and modern!'

'Well, Donna and her husband *are* separated.' Missi now sounded defensive. Defensive of whom? Brandy wondered. Donna or Mitch?

'Why doesn't she get a divorce and marry Mitchell?' Even though she hated herself for continuing the topic, Brandy had to ask.

'Beats me,' Missi shrugged. 'And everyone else that knows them. Maybe, for different reasons, they both prefer it this way.'

Luckily, at that point a window display caught Missi's attention and the conversation was dropped. At least aloud. Inside Brandy's head it revolved incessantly for the rest of the day and into the early part of the evening.

Distracted by tormenting visions of Mitch and the statuesque Donna, Brandy was only surfacely aware of her sisters' chatter during supper and the ensuing clearing away. A plaintive note in Bev's tone finally broke through to her consciousness.

'What? I'm sorry, honey, I didn't hear what you said.'

'I asked what you'd like for your birthday dinner.' Bev shook her head at Brandy's unusual behaviour.

Her birthday! Brandy stifled a gasp of surprise. How could she have forgotten her own birthday? She would be twenty-six on the coming Friday. Twenty-six—funny, she didn't feel a day over ninety-two. With difficulty she again brought her concentration back to Bev.

'What dinner?'

'The one Karen, Bev and I are going to prepare for you,' Darcy stuck her oar into the discussion. 'Is there anything in particular you're hungry for?'

'Home-made pot-pie,' Brandy replied at once, expecting, and receiving, three exaggerated groans of dismay. Before any one of them could voice a protest, Brandy gently removed the hook.

'I'm just teasing,' she soothed. 'Actually, I have a yen for meat loaf and browned potatoes, and maybe a fresh spinach salad to begin.'

A collective sigh of relief greeted her revised menu.

'*That* we can handle.' Karen spoke for the three, glancing around to receive Darcy's and Bev's nods of agreement. 'Oh, yeah,' she went on airily, 'Bev invited Mitch to help celebrate, she knew you wouldn't mind.'

Wouldn't mind? Good lord, the last person she wanted at her birthday dinner, or *any* dinner, for that matter, was Mitch Waring. Brandy was so unnerved she didn't even realise she had thought of him as Mitch. Eyeing her sisters' expectant expressions, she sighed in defeat.

'Of course I don't mind,' she lied stoutly, already dreading the meal that was still four days away.

In an effort to keep her thoughts at bay, Brandy filled the hours of those days with chores both necessary and unnecessary. Still the visions of Mitch and Donna rose to torment her.

Why should you care what he does or who he does it with? she scathingly berated herself at least a hundred times. As she persistently refused to allow an answer to form in her conscious mind, the sometimes erotic visions continued to torture her.

An unwelcome respite came in the form of another obscene call late Thursday night.

'Brandy!'

She was stepping out of the shower when she heard her name called somewhat fearfully. Pulling on a terrycloth robe, she dashed into the living room, demanding breathlessly, 'Whatever is the matter?'

Bev's face was stark with fright, her paleness accentuated in the artificial glow from the table lamp.

'Bev, honey!' Brandy exclaimed as she ran to draw the girl into the safety of her arms. 'What's wrong? Are you ill?'

Bev shook her head. 'I could be. I just answered the phone and——' she gulped—'it was that—that creep again!'

'What did he say?' Brandy demanded, anger making her voice strained.

'Yuck!' Bev spat the sound. 'I wouldn't repeat it. *He's* the one that's ill!'

'Yes.' Brandy ran her hands soothingly over the youngster's back. 'I'll call the telephone company again in the morning. Put it out of your mind, honey. I'll take care of it,' she promised grimly.

In truth, there was very little she *could* do about the calls, as she soon found out the following morning. The pleasant-voiced young woman she spoke to at the telephone company was understanding of her agitation and told her to contact her if the caller persisted. In that event, the young woman said, a special investigating team would be called in.

Frustration joined forces with apprehension to keep Brandy moving the rest of the day. As dinner time drew ever nearer, Brandy began dropping things in nervousness.

Banished from the kitchen, she went to her room to shower and change after closing the shop.

Dressed in a ruffled prairie skirt and long-sleeved blouse, she winced as she tugged her hairbrush through her loose curls and compared the far from breathtaking beauty reflected in her dresser mirror with the Amazon-sized, very beautiful Donna.

'Why should you care how you compare?' she chided the sad-eyed image. 'Or for that matter, why should it bother you to know he's involved with a married woman? He means nothing to you.' Biting her lips, she leaned closer to the mirror. 'Does he?' The sad-eyed birthday girl blinked but did not answer.

Brandy heard him as she descended the back stairway to the kitchen. His deep laughter mingled with and enhanced the young girls' giggles that filled the room. An inexplicable feeling of contentment settled on her and a soft smile curved her gloss-tinted lips. For reasons she didn't care to examine, the joyful sound wafting up the stairs to greet her seemed right and proper.

The sight that met her eyes stopped her cold on the

bottom tread. Coatless, his white shirt gleaming in the glare from the ceiling light fixture, a tea towel draped around his waist, Mitch stood at the table grinning as he crumbled slices of crisp bacon on to the deep green spinach leaves in a large wooden salad bowl.

The strange thing was, Brandy decided in that instant before her presence was realised, he did not look incongruous or out of place. In fact, he looked completely at home. One waving lock of his dark hair had fallen on to his forehead and he looked young and relaxed and heart-wrenchingly attractive.

In that instant Brandy knew she was in love for the first time in her twenty-six years of life. The knowing was more saddening then shattering. Mitchell Waring was not for her—not with a knock-out like Donna at his beck and call.

'Brandy, your timing is perfect!' Karen catching sight of her hovering at the bottom of the stairs, alerted the others to her presence. 'I was just going to call you.'

Dinner was delicious, not surprisingly since Brandy had taught all three of her sisters to cook in exactly the same way as their mother had taught her. The menu consisted of what she had requested, plus the added attraction of a large, beautifully decorated birthday cake ablaze with twenty-siz candles.

Much to her surprise the conversation flowed easily and, at times hilariously, Mitch drawing gasps of laughter from the girls as he related anecdotes of his, in his words, misspent youth.

When the table had been cleared of all but the cake and their coffee cups, Bev slipped out of her chair to dash up the back stairs. She re-entered the kitchen carrying a gaily wrapped package. As she handed Brandy the gift, she began a chorus of 'Happy Birthday to You', and was immediately joined by Karen, Darcy, and Mitch.

Flustered, more by Mitch's serenade than anything else, Brandy felt her fingers trembling as she tore away the wrapping. A small gasping 'oh' escaped her lips as she removed the beige leather bag she had admired the previous Monday in Mitch's store.

Her fingers lightly caressing the leather, Brandy breathed a choked 'thank you'. She had glanced at the price tag in the store and she knew what the bag had cost her sisters, and——

Her eyes darkened with suspicion as she shot a glance at Mitch. A tiny, negative shake of his head warned her to hold her tongue in front of the girls. His expression told her they'd discuss it later.

CHAPTER SEVEN

'OKAY, give me hell, if you feel you must, and get it over with.'

They had just entered the living room, having literally been chased out of the kitchen by the still laughing teenagers. Mitch had beaten her to the draw with his drawled invitation, for Brandy had been about to chastise him.

'Are you admitting I have the right to feel annoyed?' Brandy demanded quietly, determined to keep her voice from reaching her sisters.

'Not at all,' Mitch countered. 'I'm merely admitting I know you *are* annoyed.'

'How generous of you!' Turning away, she crossed the room and sank on to the sofa.

'Yes, isn't it?'

His obvious amusement rankled, and Brandy lifted her head to glare at him. Sitting down had been a mistake, for she had to look a long way up. How in the world had he grown so large? Had he been force-fed nothing but vitamins as a baby?

Though he had slipped on his jacket before sitting down at the dinner table, he had removed it again en route from the kitchen, tossing it over the back of a chair on entering the living room. The overall picture he presented, standing smack in the middle of the room, was knee-weakening. Running a glance over him, Brandy changed her mind—sitting down had not been a mistake, it had been a necessity.

Either he frequents a spa or health club or he spent

at least part of the winter pursuing the sun, she mused, admiring the toasty-tan colour of his skin. He works out, regularly, she decided, noting the muscular tightness of his shoulders and chest, the slimness of his waist and hips and the lack of excess flesh from neck to ankles. Much, much too virile and good-looking, she handed down her final judgment, serenely unaware of his interest-brightened hazel eyes observing every nuance of emotion playing across her expressive features. Brandy's eyes flew to his when he laughed softly.

'Well, what's the prognosis?'

'W—what?' Brandy felt her face grow warm; she knew very well 'what'. She had been staring rudely for goodness knows how many minutes.

'I feel like I've been dissected by an expert.' The beginnings of a grin split his lips. 'Will I live?' The grin was wide now and full of devilment.

Her flush deepening, Brandy stammered, 'I—I'm sorry.'

'I'm not.' His grin disappeared while his eyes seemed to darken. 'I liked the feel of your eyes on my body.'

Brandy gasped with the flash fire that shot through her veins. Even at a distance of five feet this man's effect on her was dangerously potent. Trapped, feeling herself melting under the intensity of his smouldering gaze, she cast about for an avenue of escape. In desperation, she ran down the one marked defensive anger.

'How did you manage to get yourself invited here tonight, anyway?'

'I didn't have to do a thing but be my charming self,' he mocked her puny effort. 'As a matter of fact, Bev invited me, in this very room, last Sunday night.'

Mitch paused to run a speculative glance over her. 'You do remember last Sunday night, don't you?'

Would she ever forget it? Could one forget being told their independent days were numbered? Not ready to analyse that warning, let alone discuss it, Brandy attacked from a different direction.

'I see your heavy hand in my birthday gift, too,' she tossed. 'I *saw* the price tag on that bag. There was no way the girls could have afforded it. Explain that.'

'Sure.' His shrug was eloquent. 'The bag went on sale on Tuesday.'

Outflanked, Brandy stared at him, storm clouds gathering in her eyes. When he moved across the room to her she had to clench her hands to keep from shrinking back against the sofa. Damn, the man was intimidating!

For all his lack of superfluous flesh, he had to tip the scales at thirteen stone at the very least, yet, strangely, his movements were fluidly graceful as he lowered his large frame on to the cushion beside her. With one large hand he captured both her wrists and gently, carefully loosened her tightly curled fingers.

'Lighten up, honey,' he murmured chidingly, feeling her taut resistance through her fingers. 'You saw the girls' faces. They were so damned thrilled at being able to give you something you really wanted.' His eyes searched her face consideringly. 'I'm convinced you don't mention wanting *anything* very often. Do you?'

'To what purpose?' Brandy tried, unsuccessfully, to pull her hands from his. 'Simply growing up is difficult enough, they certainly don't need feelings of guilt over my supposed sacrifices.' Becoming unnerved by the warmth spreading up her arms, she gave another tug against his grip, again unsuccessfully. 'In any case,' she went on, a little breathlessly, 'I don't feel as if I *have* made any sacrifices. My sisters hold a great deal more value than any material things could.'

'I know that.' Mitch's low tone, combined with the soothing, stroking action of his long fingers along her much smaller, slimmer ones, sent a tingle in the wake of the growing warmth. 'But in this case there *was* something, and I knew it. What harm if I made it possible for them to provide it?'

'A purely selfless act of kindness?' Brandy taunted chokingly, beginning to feel panic at the way her body was reacting to his lightly caressing touch.

'Not at all,' he contradicted, in that same low, mind-scrambling tone. 'A purely selfish act. I really like those kids. It gives me pleasure to see them happy.'

How did one argue with a statement like that? One didn't, of course. Especially if one was beginning to feel consumed by the flame leaping in a pair of hazel eyes. Brandy didn't even try. Mesmerised, shattered by the effect of his nearness, she stared, unblinking, as he slowly lowered his head to hers.

The feel of his lips drove what little sense she had retained out of her mind like a powerful drug. Mitch didn't move. Except for the light clasp of his hands and the contact of his mouth, he did not touch her. He didn't have to. The gentle motion of his mouth on hers drew her senses into an enveloping, euphoric embrace, as binding and complete as if he had crushed her to his hard body.

Drowning in the sensations flooding through her, Brandy moaned softly as she parted her lips to the exploratory probing of his. A low groan echoed her moan when she allowed him access and he deepened the kiss into a harsh demand—a demand she was dangerously close to obeying when the intrusive sound of her sisters, bantering their way up the back stairs, parted them.

'To be continued,' Mitch murmured warningly, as he drew back, releasing her hands and lips simultaneously.

For ever after, the rest of that evening would remain a hazy memory for Brandy. Bemused, lost in the wonder of Mitch's mind-divorcing kiss, most of what went on around her was muted and blurred. She knew there was a lot of laughter interspersed with the conversation, yet, although she joined in, she could not remember what they had laughed about or the actual context of the conversation.

The only clear recollection she had was of escorting Mitch to the front door somewhere around eleven, and the gleam of speculation in his eyes as he studied her face. Made nervous by his lengthy appraisal, Brandy's voice trembled as she stumbled into speech.

'Th-thank you—for helping the girls out with my present, and—and for coming, they—er—really enjoyed the evening.'

'So did I,' he returned seriously. 'Especially those few moments right before they joined us in the living room.' A small smile played across his lips. 'Your days grow even shorter, Brandy.'

Shaken, put on guard by his cool self-confidence, Brandy backed away verbally.

'Please don't read more into that——'

'I can read you like a first grade primer, Brandy,' he interrupted laughingly. 'And I'm looking forward to watching you struggle. You're independent and determined, but so am I.' His smile widened. 'And I can be *very* determined when I really want something; and I really do want you. I fully expect you to fight me every inch of the way, and I'm going to love wearing you down mentally, and then'—catching her chin in one long hand, he bent down until his face was an inch from hers—'and then I'm going to love wearing you out—physically.'

Brandy's gasp was muffled by his fast, hard kiss, and then he was gone. Teetering between longing and anger, she stared blankly at the solid wood door, blinking against the unfamiliar hot sting of tears.

During the weekend and the early part of the following week, Brandy endeavoured to come to terms with the realisation of the love she felt for Mitchell Waring. She didn't bother taxing herself with why or how it had happened. It *had* happened, and she accepted the emotion as fact. No, the mental exercise that consumed nearly every one of her waking minutes was how to handle her emotions—and him.

By late Tuesday afternoon, in all honesty, she admitted to herself that what she most longed to do was simply give up. She felt only half alive, and she knew the only place she would ever feel whole again was locked safely inside his bearlike embrace.

Merely thinking about being enfolded within his arms, crushed against his strength, caused trembling shudders. The memory of his mouth, teasing, caressing, demanding, made her ache all over with need. Fight him? Good heavens, she wanted to love him to distraction!

It was at this point that Brandy sighed with loss and defeat. He was not for her. Oh, he might want her, for the moment, very likely because she presented a challenge, but his affections were held by a tall, gorgeous, throaty-voiced blonde.

Shoulders slumping, Brandy swiped impatiently at the tears rolling slowly down her cheeks. She had no choice, she *had* to fight him, keep her guard up at all times, because she knew, without doubt, that should he even suspect the depths of her feelings for him he would not hesitate a second; he would annihilate her— at least emotionally.

Her decision to stand and defend was put to the test that very evening.

The moment the dishes were dispensed with, the table cleared of supper clutter, Darcy plonked a textbook on to the smooth top.

'Mitch is coming over to help me with my maths homework,' she announced, somewhat triumphantly.

Standing at the sink, wringing out a sodden dishcloth, Brandy turned slowly to stare at Darcy. 'Mitch is going to do—what?' she asked with forced calmness, suddenly wishing it was *his* neck she was twisting.

'He's coming over to help me with my maths,' Darcy repeated smugly.

'How and when did you manage to talk him into that?' Bev demanded, her tone betraying envy.

'I didn't have to talk him into anything,' Darcy denied vehemently. 'He stopped in at the insurance office this afternoon to see how I was getting on, and, as business was slow to stop, he caught me struggling over my homework. He offered to come to the house tonight and help me, I didn't ask him.'

'I wonder if he knows French?' Karen murmured consideringly.

'Or English grammar?' Bev groaned.

'Now, wait a minute!' Dropping the cloth into the sink, Brandy made a full turn, hands on hips. 'I don't want you girls imposing on Mitchell Waring's time,' she ordered loudly. 'Is that understood?'

'Yes, Mommie.'

Brandy's head swivelled to the source of that teasing

drawl, to find Mitch's form filling the space created by the door being silently pushed open.

'I was about to knock when I heard my name mentioned,' he explained. 'May I come in?'

Silly question. Brandy frowned at the uproar of squealed greetings her sisters gave by way of an answer. How had Mitch managed to become such a hero to the girls in such a short amount of time? Another silly question. Hadn't she lost her heart, and most of her common sense, to him in the same amount of time?

En garde! The warning flashed through Brandy's mind as he strolled into the room, confidence stamped indelibly on his bearing.

'Thanks, gang,' his glance encompassed the adoring-faced teenagers. 'I love you, too.'

Brandy choked back a gasp of pain his avowal sent piercing through her. Dear God, what would she do to hear him say those words to her in that tone of utter conviction? She knew the answer to that; she would do almost anything.

The knowledge of exactly how far gone on him she was set off an alarm in her head. She was going to have to be very, very careful. Schooling her features, she faced him squarely when he turned to her.

'Good evening, Brandy.' The caressing quality of his tone undermined her determination, which, judging from the gleam in his eyes, had obviously been his intention. 'Did I detect a note of disapproval in your voice?' At her questioning expression, he clarified, 'About me helping Darcy with her homework.'

'No, of course not.' Brandy dismissed the idea with an idle wave of her hand, as if his being there was of no importance to her one way or the other. 'I just don't want any of the girls imposing on you.'

'No imposition at all.' Mitch's lips smiled. His eyes called her a faker. 'As a matter of actual fact'—he glanced at Darcy, lifting one dark brow in an exaggerated arch—'I am very good with figures.'

'I'll bet you are,' Karen giggled, picking up on his double entendre.

'Yeah, but are you any good with English grammar?' Bev demanded, impervious to his word play.

'English grammar!' Mitch exclaimed, over-dramatically. 'Are you kidding? I are a whizz!'

Darcy collapsed on to a kitchen chair in a fit of laughter. Karen's hand flew to her mouth to stifle her giggles. Ever spontaneous, Bev ran across the room to fling herself into his arms, her small body shaking with mirth.

Lifting her eyes ceilingward, Brandy turned back to the sink—only then allowing a smile to smooth her pursed lips. Had she really, only moments ago, been wondering how he had wormed his way into their affections?

With three teenage girls and one very large, mature man parked around the table, the homework session began.

With patient forbearance, Mitch explained, demonstrated and, in effect, presented the key that unlocked the mathematical mystery for Darcy.

'My gosh!' an awed Darcy cried. 'Why couldn't my teacher make it that clear?'

'He, or she, probably could,' Mitch chided. '*If* he, or she, had an equal amount of time to spend on each individual student.'

'Okay,' Darcy grinned her understanding, 'I can dig that.'

'I thought you might,' he drawled. 'Now, shall we make a foray into the intricacies of English grammar?'

It was at this point that Brandy absented herself from the makeshift classroom.

Curling into a corner of the sofa near a reading lamp, she picked up a paperback romance. Despite no lack of talent of the book's author, she let the slim volume drop into her lap after reading the first page for the third time without absorbing its contents.

Was Mitch, she wondered disconcertedly, ingratiating himself with her sisters to gain her approval, and subsequent favour? With a sharp shake of her head she rejected the notion at once. The picture simply didn't fit with the man's emerging personality. Brandy felt certain that had he felt no sympathy whatever for the girls he would have coolly tolerated them while going about his stated business of wearing her down. The fact that he did obviously like them made it doubly hard for her to withstand his campaign.

Closing her eyes, Brandy re-enacted the tutoring session she had finally had to escape from. At one point, at an impish remark from Bev, Mitch had let loose a bark of laughter that had resounded around the room, drawing reciprocative laughter from his delighted devotees.

Brandy's heart contracted at the memory of that joyful sound, the carefree, almost boyish expression on his face. Had she really, on first sight, judged him not handsome? Her mind boggled at her own blindness. Mitchell Waring was *the* most attractive man she'd ever had the pleasure—misfortune?—of meeting.

Careful, girl, she warned herself shakily. If you keep on in this vein, *he* won't have to do a damn thing, you'll lose this war by default.

Her resolutions reaffirmed, Brandy contrived to throw up roadblocks to his attempts at making inroads against her defences later that night, and when he just happened to drop in on Wednesday and Thursday evenings.

She was standing at the bottom of the front stairs after seeing Mitch out on Wednesday night, trying to normalise her breathing, made erratic by side-stepping his searching mouth, when the phone rang. She heard Karen answer 'Hello', then the slamming of the receiver and a shrilly cried, 'Pig!'

Not again! Running up the stairs, Brandy dashed into the living room, to find Karen standing by the telephone, white-faced and trembling.

'That man is an absolute pig!' she choked around a sob. 'Brandy, can't something be done to stop him? God, you have to be afraid to answer your own phone! Besides being disgusting, it's frightening!' The fear was all too evident in the eyes she turned to Brandy.

Frustrated anger surged through Brandy. Damn this—this animal! Her protective juices running fierce and hot, she crossed the room to Karen and, as she had the week before with Bev, drew her into her arms.

'I'll call the phone company again tomorrow morning, raise some hell,' Brandy promised soothingly. 'Maybe I can set a fire under somebody and get some action.'

'Well, I hope they can catch him soon—these calls are beginning to give us all the creeps.' Karen sniffed. 'We were talking about it after Bev answered last week and——' she paused, then asked fearfully, 'You don't think he could be watching the house, do you, Brand?'

Brandy bit back a groan of dismay. Could he? The idea that their sinister caller might be watching the house was no more upsetting than the realisation of how frightened her sisters were.

'I doubt it, honey.' She didn't doubt it at all, but she had to try to reassure Karen. Apparently she was not completely successful.

'Well, even so,' Karen blinked, fighting tears, 'I'm glad we're going to Gram's tomorrow for the weekend. At least we won't have to jump every time the phone rings. I only wish you were going too.'

'You know I have to be here at the store.' Brandy closed the shop at five every day but Friday; that night the store was open until nine. 'I'll be perfectly all right.'

At five o'clock the following afternoon, Brandy stuck the Back-in-one-hour sign in the display window, then, after stowing her sisters and their overnight cases into the car, she drove them to their grandparents' home on the outskirts of the city.

On the way back to the shop she pulled into the drive-in window of a fast food restaurant to order a cheeseburger and Coke for her supper. An hour later she was wondering why she had rushed, as she hadn't had one customer in the store. Come to that, she might as well have given in to her grandmother's coaxing when she'd talked to her on the phone earlier in the week.

'It will be lovely having the girls here for the weekend, but I do wish you'd consider closing the shop and staying over with them. You work too hard, Brandy.'

Straightening already neatly arranged shelves, Brandy smiled as her grandmother's plea drifted through her mind. The temptation to close the shop early and run to her grandmother's home where she would be petted and cosseted was suddenly very strong. How heavenly it would be to snuggle into her grandfather's arms, rest her head on his shoulder.

With a sigh, Brandy dismissed the temptation. Her grandparents were having problems of their own making ends meet in their retirement, and though she knew they would both go without to help her, she also knew she would never ask their help, either emotional or financial.

Brandy sighed again, her fingertips trailing over the lacy wax finish of one of her most popular creations. It *would* be nice to creep into a strong pair of arms, shift her problems on to a pair of broad shoulders, if only for a little while, but her grandfather's arms were not all that strong any more, and his shoulders were slightly stooped.

Her fingers stilled on the candle as a vision of an enormous pair of shoulders, long arms steely with strength, danced tormentingly into her mind. Those arms could give protection as well as comfort. Those shoulders could take the weight of her burdens without feeling the pressure. They had been offered to her, those arms and shoulders. All she had to give in return was her independence; her determination, her pride, her self.

A shudder rippled through her body, causing her hand to shake so badly she almost knocked the expensive candle off the shelf. Her hand dropping limply to her side, Brandy closed her eyes. God! She wanted to give in, crawl into the haven of his arms and lose herself there.

With a sharp shake of her head, she turned away from the row of shelves. The price was too high. Oh, not the physical price. She would eagerly pay that, revelling every minute in the sensuous joy of being united with the man she had suddenly found herself in love with. No, it was not the physical aspect that terrified her. It was the knowledge of what that union would do to her emotionally that made her hold herself aloof.

When he had appeased his appetite for her, tossed

her aside for someone new, more exciting, she would be left shattered, useless, and she knew it. Brandy didn't even know how she knew it, but she was positive that, once belonging to Mitchell Waring, she would never again be able to tolerate another man.

Fingernails digging into her palms, her teeth punishing her lower lip, Brandy spun around. She *had* to stop thinking of him, longing for him. Her shifting glance settled on the clock. Eight forty-seven. The hell with it! She was going to close the shop and go have a long, hot soak in the tub.

She had taken two steps in the direction of the front door when the phone rang, and she veered to the counter-desk and lifted the receiver. As it was the ring for her home number and not for the business, she merely said:

'Hello?'

A finger of ice slithered down her back when a raspy, male voice insinuated:

'Do you know what I'd like to do to you?'

Going cold all over, Brandy pulled the receiver away from her ear, only vaguely hearing the words that followed. It was the same man who had been frightening her sisters. Goddamn him!

Her arm moved to slam the receiver on to its cradle, and at that instant pure, blind rage exploded throughout her entire being. This man had to be stopped, and if the phone company couldn't stop him, then *she* would!

Not pausing to think, Brandy brought the receiver back to her ear.

'What did you have in mind, honey?' Had that sultry voice really come out of *her* throat? Brandy wondered in amazement.

There was a brief pause, and then the male voice,

oily now, went on to describe in graphic detail exactly what he had in mind. Her cheeks paling, her eyes widening in shock, Brandy listened to the disgusting suggestions until she felt her stomach turn, then, in an attempt to silence him she drawled:

'Promises, promises.'

'You think so, baby?' The oily voice held a touch of belligerence, and perhaps a shading of bravado. 'Meet me somewhere and I'll show *you*.'

The shading of bravado made Brandy pause. Could it be possible that this man was not as sure of himself as he would have her believe? Decision was not a conscious thing.

'All right,' she blurted. 'Where?'

He named the parking lot of a supermarket that Brandy was unfamiliar with on the outer fringes of the city.

'Okay, I'll be there,' Brandy shocked herself by replying, 'but I can't get there before ten.'

'That's good, the store will be closed by then. I—I can't wait.'

Neither can I, Brandy thought grimly as she heard the click as he disconnected, and then the dial tone buzz, but I won't be alone!

She did not realise she was holding the receiver in mid-air, nor did she hear the chime of the small bells fastened to the inside of the front door. As to that, she wasn't even aware that she was shaking all over, or of the starkness of her expression.

'Brandy?'

The note of concern in the deep voice didn't register.

'What the devil?' Strong fingers pried her death grip from the receiver. 'Brandy, are you ill?' The receiver crashed against the cradle. 'Answer me! What's wrong? Who were you talking to?'

Blinking, Brandy lifted her head just as Mitch's hands grasped her shoulders.

'Oh, Mitch!' Reaction beginning to set in, she felt her legs buckle at the realisation of what she had just agreed to. 'Oh, Mitch,' she whispered. Had his hold on her not tightened, she would have crumpled to the floor at his feet.

'Damn it, Brandy, who was that on the phone?' Mitch's voice was strained with impatience, and a touch of fear. 'Was it something about the girls?'

'No, no,' Brandy shook her head. 'It—it was that man. You know, the obscene caller.'

'And?' Mitch's jaw set, almost as if he knew her answer was not going to please him.

'And I——' Brandy wetted suddenly parched lips, then blurted, 'And I agreed to meet him tonight.'

'You—did—what?' he breathed in a deadly harsh tone. If the sound of his voice was frightening, and it was, his face was even more so.

'He has to be stopped!' Brandy cried, attempting to escape his bruising clasp.

'Not by you!' he exclaimed roughly.

'Who, then?' Brandy demanded. 'Oh, I know the phone company's men are doing their best,' she rushed on, 'but who knows how long it will take? Meanwhile, the girls are actually terrified every time the phone rings.' She drew a deep breath before reiterating, 'He has to be stopped.'

'Brandy, this clown is very likely a few crackers shy of a full box.' His hands shook her shoulders lightly. 'You are *not* going to meet him.'

The nerve of him! Gritting her teeth, Brandy stared straight into his frosty eyes. 'I am not stupid, Mitchell,' she enunciated clearly. 'I was not going to meet him alone. I'm going to call the police to meet me there.'

'And the minute he sees the patrol car he'll take off,' he taunted harshly. 'Forget it, Brandy.'

'No!' Twisting her shoulders, she wrenched away from him. 'You don't know what his calls have done to the girls,' she accused as she went to lock the door. 'He's going to be stopped, if I have to do it myself.' The bolt slamming into place punctuated her vow.

'Okay.'

Her eyes wary, Brandy turned away from the door to face him. He had given in too easily, much too easily.

'You won't try to stop me?' Perversely, Brandy felt let down.

'No.'

'But . . .'

'I'm going with you.'

Trying to ignore the thrill his possessive tone sent coursing through her, she began to protest.

'But if he sees a man in the car with me he'll take off as fast as he would on seeing a patrol car!'

'He won't see me.' A tiny non-smile tugged his tautened lips. 'Don't argue, Brandy. I'm going with you.'

CHAPTER EIGHT

BRANDY'S nervous perspiration-moist palms gripped the unfamiliar steering wheel. On leaving the house a few minutes ago, Mitch had led her away from her own small car and in the direction of a long dark Lincoln Continental parked at the kerb a short distance away from the shop.

Strangely, her nervousness was not caused by the coming confrontation with the man who had until now been a disembodied, frightening voice on the phone. The fear of that meeting had vanished with Mitch's grimly stated, 'I'm going with you.'

What had her nervous now was the fear of doing something stupid and in some way damaging Mitch's showroom-new car. It was an expensively plush beauty and, although she was a careful, experienced driver, small knots had started gathering in her stomach the moment he had casually handed her the keys.

'You drive very well, if a little slow,' his soft, teasing voice crept to her from where he had ensconced himself on the back seat.

Not for the world would she admit to him that being behind the wheel of his new toy filled her with tension.

'I'm pacing myself to arrive at the parking lot as close to ten as possible.' Her explanation, tossed coolly over her shoulder, was met with a low, derisive chuckle. 'We're almost there now,' she went on, ignoring his amusement. 'Hadn't you better get into position?'

Mitch didn't reply, but she heard him shuffling about in the back and she had to swallow a bubble of laughter as she pictured him folding his large frame into the relatively small amount of floor space between the front and back seats.

The bubble of laughter grew as she heard him grumbling, and nearly escaped when he gave a grunted yelp of pain.

'Comfy, Mitch?' she asked sweetly.

'Shut up and drive!' His growled warning threatened to release her mirth and Brandy had to bite her lip to contain it. 'I hope you realise you're going to pay for the discomfort I'm suffering now?' His gently murmured taunt sent her giggles scurrying, to be replaced by a confusion of feelings, the uppermost being excitement.

Fortunately, she was spared the task of sorting out her confusing emotions as at that moment she approached the intersection where the supermarket was located.

'We're here,' she advised him through dry lips. 'The parking lot appears to be empty.' Drawing a shaky breath, she croaked, 'What if he doesn't show?' This last was whispered as she drove to one corner of the lot. Killing the powerful engine, she tugged on the handbrake and sat perfectly still.

'Patience, little girl.'

A tingle shivered along the outside of Brandy's arms. The reaction was not from his chiding tone, but from the context of his jibe. Never before had a man called her 'little girl'. At five feet, five and a half inches, she was not a small woman, except perhaps in comparison to the man-mountain, Mitchell Waring!

Brandy felt as if she should feel patronised, or put down, or *something*. Conversely, what she was experiencing was a bemusing feeling of being cherished, looked after, cared for.

Her bemusement was shattered as the glare from a pair of headlights illuminated the interior of the car for an instant as another vehicle drove on to the large, dimly lighted parking lot.

'There's a car!' Brandy squeaked on a gulp. 'One occupant,' she breathed. 'It's a man. He's parking. He's getting out and walking this way!' She was finding it increasingly more difficult to control her voice. 'My God!' a faint whisper now, 'he's little more than a boy, seventeen, eighteen at most.'

'Steady, sweetheart.' Mitch's cautioning murmur had the desired effect. Amazingly, Brandy felt suddenly very calm.

The window beside her was at half-mast, and when the young man was still some four or five feet from the car she heard the now too familiar voice of their telephone tormentor.

'You're beautiful!' The oily voice held astonishment. 'Much better looking even than I'd pictured you from your voice.'

At his first unwanted compliment, Brandy whispered, 'It's him,' through lips that barely moved.

By the time the young man had finished speaking he was less than a foot from the car, his voice clear in the silent night air. A tiny frown creased Brandy's brow at the sound of a muttered, obscene oath from behind her, then she jerked erect in surprise as the rear door was flung open and Mitch exploded on to the macadam from his crouched hiding place.

'You son-of-a——!' his voice held both shock and fury. 'Sammy! What in *hell* do you think you're doing?' One very long arm shot out, and one very large hand grabbed a hold the boy's tee-shirt.

'Mr Waring?'

'You know him?'

The young man's and Brandy's voices meshed in astonished unison, the young man's in fear, Brandy's in surprise.

'I know his parents,' Mitch growled, nearly lifting the tall, slender youth off his feet while administering a rough shake. 'I play racquet ball with his father twice a week—he's a very prominent man in this area. If word of this gets out——' he shook the youth again. 'What the hell *do* you think you're doing?'

The boy, for Brandy could see now that he was still a boy, about Darcy's age, already pale, went sheet-white at Mitch's enraged tone.

'I—I didn't mean——' the boy swallowed with obvious difficulty. 'I—I wasn't going to really *do* anything,' he finished on a wail.

'You weren't going to get the opportunity,' Mitch snarled, flinging him towards the gaping back of the car. 'Get in!'

'Wh-where are you taking me?' The threat of tears trembled on the edge of the boy's voice. 'Are you going to turn me in?'

'I should.' Mitch followed the boy on to the back seat, slamming the door behind him. 'But I won't.' Brandy heard the boy sigh with relief, then gasp as Mitch added, 'I'm escorting you directly to your father.'

'He'll kill me!' The boy's voice was shrill with fear.

'Tough.' Mitchell's tone held cruel unconcern. 'Drive, Brandy, I'll direct you as we go.'

'Mr Waring, please, don't tell my dad! I promise you——'

Brandy heard the soft plea as she switched on the engine. A shiver went through her body when Mitch's deadly soft voice cut him off.

'Shut your mouth, or I'll shut it for you. You deserve a good beating, and I hope your father has the guts to administer it!'

Following Mitch's terse directions, Brandy drove to an exclusively residential neighbourhood, pulling into the long, curving driveway he indicated.

'Brandy?' Mitch's voice prompted her when she made no move to get out after bringing the car to a halt.

Brandy had been through an interview with Mitchell Waring not too unlike the one forthcoming. She did not relish a repeat performance, even one where she would not be on the receiving end. 'I'll wait here for you.' The finality in her tone stopped his hand as he reached for the door release. His hand hovered in mid-air a moment, then dropped to his side.

'Right, I won't be long.' Turning away, he gave young Sammy a nudge to get him moving. 'Lock the doors,' he ordered over his shoulder as he strode, Sammy in tow, towards the large house.

After securing the locks, Brandy slid from behind the wheel to the passenger's side of the bench seat. Hands clasped tightly in her lap, she shook all over as tremors of reaction racked her body. She had been precipitate in making an assignation with her unknown caller. Had Mitch not shown up at the shop when he had, it might have been a much different story. Pitted against the towering bulk of Mitchell Waring, Sammy had appeared meekly insignificant, but, faced with a lone young woman, he might have played the role of devouring predator. The suspicion that she was in for a tongue-lashing from Mitch before this long night finally came to an end, doubled the shudders attacking her.

As she sat waiting, waiting, a subtle change stole over Brandy. The tremors subsided, then ceased entirely. As calmness returned resentment reared its ugly little head. Why *should* she have to endure a tongue-lashing from Mitch? Who asked for his interference anyway? She had never even considered going to meet the caller alone. She *would* have called the police to accompany her. Did he think she was a complete fool?

Waiting, waiting, her thoughts churned on incessantly. He had been poking his nose into her affairs ever since he had brought Darcy home in disgrace. He practically had all three of her sisters eating out of his hand like trained seals! In his arrogance, he had even had the gall to warn her that she was his next victim! How *could* she have been so stupid as to fall in love with him? A memory flash of him shaking Sammy as if the boy had no more substance than a rag doll skipped through her mind. The man was not only domineering, he was a brute!

Well, no, thank you, Mr Mitchell Waring. I may be in love, but I'm not permanently out to lunch. If you think I'm going to sit quiet, head hanging abjectly, while you launch a severe chastisement, you can take a flying leap into outer space!

Completely gone were her earlier feelings of being cherished, cared for, looked after. She didn't *need* looking after, she told herself sternly. She was twenty-six, for heaven's sake! Most definitely, she didn't need one domineering, overbearing, arrogant Mitchell Waring, pursuer of married women, to tell her when to come and when to go; when to speak and when to be silent, when to *anything*, for that matter.

By the time Mitch returned to the car Brandy had worked herself up into a seething mass of mutinous outrage. When he had the temerity to glance at her questioningly after settling himself behind the wheel, she angled her chin and glared at him defiantly.

'Like that, is it?' His dryly drawled observation increased her determination to put this man in his place.

'Don't start on me, Waring,' Brandy gritted warningly.

'Waring?' One dark eyebrow arched quizzingly. 'Waring?' he repeated softly. 'Be careful, sweetie, you're tampering with a very short fuse here.'

'I'm terrified,' Brandy retorted, somehow contriving a bored tone. 'I'd like to go home now—*please*. I'm tired and I'd like to go to bed.' She knew her phrasing had been a mistake the instant the words passed her lips.

'Is that an invitation?' His brow arched higher. 'Because if it is,' he went on before she could gasp a denial, 'I accept.'

Angry words strangling her, Brandy stared at him in impotent fury. Damn him! Damn her own crazy emotions as well, for excitement at the prospect of his suggestion threatened to overrun her anger. Fighting herself, praying for the strength to fight him, she turned away in deliberate dismissal to stare stonily through the windshield.

'Will you please start this tank in disguise and take me home?'

'To bed?' he taunted, obviously surpressing laughter. 'I'd be delighted!'

Brandy's gaze jerked to the window beside her. She would *not* give him further amusement by arguing. In fact, she would not even answer him if he spoke to her again.

He didn't. Through the long minutes of the short

drive to her home Mitch didn't utter word one. Contrarily, instead of satisfaction Brandy suffered a growing feeling of frustration.

When he pulled the long car into the kerb one pavement removed from the shop, then switched off the engine, Brandy's frustration overflowed in the icy dismissal.

'Thank you for your—unsolicited—help tonight.' Swinging the car door open, she presented a rigidly controlled expression to him. 'It's unnecessary for you to see me to the door. Good ni——' she broke off as, Mitch having coolly ignored her while getting out his side, she found herself addressing an empty seat.

Telling herself the satisfaction of strangling him would be worth risking incarceration, Brandy scrambled out of the car, slammed the door, and went trailing after him.

In five years, Brandy had never been able to approach the front of her home without pausing to admire the wooden sign that hung suspended from an iron brace over the entranceway. The sign bore the handpainted likeness of a burning candle, grey smoke swirling to write out the word Candleglow in a rainbow arch over the flame.

Tonight, the sign Missi had laboured over with all her considerable skill went unnoticed for the very first time. Stamping by the large man standing in a relaxed pose to one side of the blatantly red door, Brandy thrust the key into the lock, gave it a vicious turn, then pushed the door inwards before swinging around to send him on his way.

'I'm coming in,' Mitch told her as she parted her lips to issue a brief goodnight.

'I don't——'

'I know you don't,' he blandly cut into her attempt at protest. 'But I'm coming in just the same.'

Moving towards her, he backed her into the house, closing the door with a decisive snap when he had cleared the threshold.

'Mitchell, I'm becoming very annoyed——'

This time it was his laughter that cut her off in mid-spate.

'When you're furious with me, I'm Waring. When you're annoyed with me, I'm Mitchell. When you're merely tolerating me, I'm Mitch.' A speculative gleam shimmered in his eyes. 'What, I wonder, would you call me if you came to care for me? It would be worth hanging around to find out.'

'You don't have that many years left,' Brandy retorted. 'Why did you insist on coming in?'

'For a cup of coffee,' Mitch replied smoothly, then, his lips parting in a false smile, he warned, 'And to give you hell, of course.'

'I'll make the coffee for you.' Swinging away, Brandy walked through the shop, dimly lighted at night by low wattage bulbs concealed in the ceiling. Hearing his tread close behind her, she increased her pace—even though she knew there would be no escaping his anger.

What an actor, and what a fool she'd been to be taken in by his attitude of amused tolerance. His parody of a smile, that had more the look of a snarl, had given him away. Oh yes, Mitchell Waring was one very angry man.

Going into the kitchen, Brandy scooped the electric percolator off the counter top and made a beeline for the sink. Her hand was arrested as she reached for the cold-water tap.

'Leave that for now.'

The soft command sent a shiver inching up her spine. Willing her hands to steadiness, she carefully placed the coffee pot in the plastic dish rack before slowly turning to face him.

'I thought you wanted coffee?'

'What I want is to shake you senseless!' In fury, every trace of amber fled from his eyes, leaving them a glittering green.

'You wouldn't!' she exclaimed, not at all sure of the assertion even as she voiced it.

'No, I wouldn't,' he concurred harshly. 'It would be an exercise in pointlessness anyway, as you display very little sense at all.' His narrowed eyes swept over her contemptuously. 'I swear you should be collared and put on a lead—with very little slack.' Moving slowly, he crossed the tiled floor to her. 'And the end of that lead should be placed in very firm hands.'

'Like yours, I suppose?' Brandy sneered, goaded beyond caution. Never, not even in her teens, had she been accused of lacking sense.

'Not *like* mine,' Mitch corrected her scathingly. 'Only mine. You need protection from yourself, Brandy. I think you'd better marry me.'

Shock waves tore through Brandy's body, shaking her so badly she had to grope behind her and grasp the sink to keep from falling down. Yet what shook her the most was the leaping throb of her heartbeat and pulses with an emotion that felt suspiciously like sheer joy. Calling herself a total madwoman, she gathered her puny defences and launched an attack.

'Marry *you*? Are you out of your over-inflated head?'

'Not at all.' His eyes assessed her thoughtfully. 'As a matter of fact, I think it's the most logical solution.'

'As a matter of fact,' she parroted sarcastically, 'I

think *you're* a few crackers shy of a full box. And, if I may be so brash as to ask, logical solution to exactly—what?'

'Why, all your problems,' he smiled, sweetly.

'What problems?' she smiled back nastily.

'Emotional. Physical. Financial,' Mitch enumerated.

'I have no emotional problems,' she lied bravely. 'And you're the one with a physical problem. Even though why you should be with——' Brandy caught herself just in time. His affair with the statuesque Donna really was none of her business, even if it did hurt like hell.

'With—what?' he rapped, the picture of innocent confusion.

Brandy shook her head. She had to back off of that subject. 'Nothing—I—what do you mean, financial? Have you been pumping the girls again?'

'Still,' he corrected. 'Business hasn't picked up the way you hoped it would, has it?'

'No.' He already knew the answer, why bother lying?

He was too close now, much too close. With the sink digging a groove into the small of her back, Brandy had no form of retreat. In truth she didn't want to retreat. She wanted to advance, to slide her arms around his surprisingly trim waist and lie against the solid living wall of his chest. In an effort to combat the desire to surrender draining her limbs of strength, Brandy's grip tightened on the edge of the old porcelain sink.

'How long can you go on fighting?'

Startled, Brandy's eyes flickered to his. Had her face revealed her inner battle to him? The glow of victory she expected to see lighting his features was not there. A sigh of relief whispered through her lips when he went on:

'It can only be a matter of weeks before your back's to the wall. Then what will you do? Mortgage this place to the hilt? Lose the shop you've put so much time, energy and talent into?' Mitch's hard-eyed gaze pierced hers. 'And for what? To salvage your pride and independence?' His voice was strained with—what? impatience? frustration? 'Pride and independence will be meagre fare when the cupboards are empty.' He was less than half a foot from her now, his tone soft, cajoling. 'Give it up, Brandy. Accept my proposal.'

Oh, how she longed to accept, ached to accept. Mitchell Waring, her husband! A delicious tingle sensitised her skin. Brandy clamped her lips together to bar the impulsive yes that rushed to her mouth. Aligning herself with him would be like walking a balancing line on a two-edged sword. The one edge capable of cutting through her self erected barriers to expose her to ecstasy. The other edge able to slash deeply to inflict agony. Could she walk that delicate line?

This time Mitch did sense the battle raging within. His voice gentle, he tried to tip the scale in his favour.

'Give it up, Brandy. I'm a great deal stronger than you. Let me shoulder at least half the weight.'

He was so close now his warm breath caressed her forehead, feathered the loose dark curls that rested there. Brandy swallowed painfully against the moan filling her throat. For an instant she teetered on the brink of capitulation, then fear gripped her mind. No, no, she couldn't! That balancing line was too delicate, too fine. She could slip, she knew it, and the slashing edge would strike, plunging her into desolation. In sheer desperation, she counter-attacked.

'I don't need or want your patronage!'

'Patronage?—what?' Mitch exhaled the words on a note of confusion. Confusion fled before the onrush of hard anger. 'Who the hell's offering patronage? I'm offering to share the weight—on an equal footing.'

'Expecting nothing in return,' Brandy forced a sneer to her soft lips. God, it hurt to fight him.

'I said equal,' Mitch retorted at once. 'Of course, I expect something in return.'

Even though she knew too well, she couldn't resist taunting, 'And that is?'

'You know damned well what *that* is.' Leaning back, he swept her form with an encompassing glance.

'The use of my body,' Brandy defined, swaying between despair and fury. 'On a fairly regular basis.'

'The use of your body,' Mitch concurred on an oddly soft, tight note, as if the effort to speak hurt his throat. 'On a *very* regular basis.'

'Share the weight! Equal footing!' Hurt beyond thinking, Brandy flung the phrases back in his face. 'Platitudes!' she accused. 'The correct word, Mr Waring, is lust.'

'What's wrong with the word lust, *Ms Styer*?' Mitch enquired with deceptive smoothness.

'It's—It's immoral!' Brandy cried out the first coherent thought that sprang to mind.

'Wrong,' he pronounced flatly.

'B—but——'

'If a man lies near death, yet clings on tenaciously, one might say he has a lust for life. Is that immoral?'

'No, but——'

'If a man propels himself into space to explore the universe and search for possible new worlds, one might say he has a lust for adventure. Is that immoral?'

'No! But that's not the same.' Brandy was surprised

she'd been allowed to finish a whole sentence. With the weapon of accusation, she made to vanquish him. 'What you're proposing is prompted by the lust for nothing but sex.'

'Wrong again.' Mitch smiled gently at the confusion she could not mask. 'Now, were I to pounce, with the intent to ravish, on any presentable female who happened to drift within my radius, then you could accuse me of having a lust for sex. But that's not the case, is it?' His smile deepened. 'No, Ms Styer, I do not lust for sex, I lust for *you*.'

Wide-eyed, feeling herself the vanquished, Brandy stared into Mitch's laughing eyes. She was going to lose this war! There was no way he could be defeated. His weaponry of words, emotions, sheer masculine magnetism was too strong for her puny defences. She was going to lose!

The certainty thrilled and dismayed her, both at the same time, but she was not yet ready to hoist the white flag. Tin, not steel, backed her decision. It was only a matter of time. Brandy now faced that fact. Yet, yet—damned if she'd allow him an easy conquest! It might well be her final gasp of defiance but, by the time he claimed the field, Mitchell Waring would know he had earned the victor's spoils.

'Brandy.' Mitch's near-groan scattered her bemused, confusing thoughts. As she lifted her lowered lashes, her eyes were filled with his visage drawing closer, closer.

'Oh, God, Brandy,' he breathed against her lips, 'give it up.'

Brandy parted her lips, but protest was made impossible as his mouth touched, then pressed, then crushed demandingly against hers.

Her backing of tin, so hastily forged, melted just as

hastily under one blast of his fire. Feeling her begin to soften, Mitch moved his body to hers, pinning her lower half to the sink. His hands touched her waist briefly, then his arms encircled her tightly. What sounded like a growl rumbled from his throat as the increased pressure from his devouring mouth forced her head way back. The action lifted her toes off the floor, leaving her see-sawing, the base of her spine the only part of her making contact with the smooth porcelain.

Again he moved. One large hand sliding to the small of her back, his hard thighs brushed the soft insides of hers.

Nearly mindless with the sensations storming her senses from his hungry mouth and roving hands, Brandy became electrified when the lower part of his body made contact with her own.

The degree of his arousal was unquestionable. The degree of his control was in doubt.

Her hands, up till now flailing the air, grasped his waist to push him away. Her fingers gripped, hesitated, then, beginning to burn from the fire coursing through her veins, joined forces at the middle of his back to urge him nearer still.

This is madness, the last, tiny lucid bit of her reasoning mind warned weakly. Will you look at yourself, the tiny portion grew in size and volume. Wantonly embracing him with arms *and* legs, while perched on the rim of—of all things—the kitchen sink!

Made uncomfortable by her own chiding conscience, Brandy writhed, innocently eliciting another deep groan from Mitch.

His mouth left hers to sample the taste of the velvety soft skin of her neck. His tongue plumbed the hollow behind her small ear, his teeth nipped at her delicate lobe, his hands stroked her back from shoulders to waist and, all the while, his hips rotated slowly, enticingly against hers.

Stop him, the tiny voice of reason ordered shrilly. You must stop him at once! Part of her wanted to obey reason's plea. Part of her wanted to break free of its restrictions, bask in the heat of his sensual caresses. Her mental struggle produced a sobbing whimper.

It was not until later that Brandy was to realise her humiliating whimper had been her salvation.

On hearing and misinterpreting it, Mitch loosened his hold to lean back and look at her, his hazel eyes bright with triumph.

'You're as hungry for me as I am for you,' he said hoarsely. 'You suffer the same affliction I do.' Even though the leaping flame in his eyes gave her warning, Brandy felt flayed by his indictment. 'Good, old-fashioned lust.'

Now the whimper was deeply embedded inside— soundless, voiceless, and all the more painful for being so. Something shrivelled and died in her being. Hope? Joy? Innocence? Anger rushed to fill the void of their passing.

She loved this man. More than her precious sisters. More than her own life! She had so very much to offer him. Truth. Loyalty. Her untouched self. Yet all he required of her was the use of her body—on a very regular basis!

Dear God, the pain was smothering. From some unknown source, strength flowed into her arms and with a bitter cry she pushed him back and away from her.

'I think I could learn to hate you, Mitch.'

'What the hell!' Mitch's face mirrored startled disbelief. 'Brandy, don't deny you wanted me moments ago.'

'I don't deny it.' Unable to meet his steady gaze, Brandy lowered her lashes.

'Then why have you introduced the word hate?' he demanded harshly. 'Do you really prefer that to lust?' His voice now held a grating quality that scraped over Brandy's overworked emotions. 'Lust is a healthy, robust word. Hate is a destructive one.'

'I know,' she admitted distractedly.

'Do you truly wish my destruction?'

In her distraction, and with her lashes still lowered, Brandy missed the odd inflection in his tone, the spasm of pain that passed fleetingly over his face. Still, the question brought shame and she shook her head.

'Do you?'

She was beyond fathoming his reason, or need for a verbal response, but she heard the hard demand for one.

'No,' a dry whisper then, stronger, 'no, of course not.'

Mitch took a step towards her and she backed up, halfway across the room.

'You're afraid.' The strain was gone from his face and voice. 'Of yourself as much as me, I think.' He smiled, so tenderly Brandy felt a throb in her throat. 'You're going to accept me, eventually. I know it, and you know it. But you have a strong streak of Pennsylvania Dutch bullheadedness, and it's having its way with you right now.'

A smile twitched his lips as he lifted his arms and held them out to her.

'Come here, stubborn one,' he invited beguilingly.

Brandy amazed herself when she moved unhesitatingly towards him. Mere minutes ago she had literally flung herself away from those same beckoning arms.

Mere minutes ago those arms represented a prison, now they held the lure of a haven.

A soft sigh trembled off her tongue as they closed around her; not too tightly, nor too loosely.

'I've fought you to a standstill,' Mitch murmured into her hair, 'and still you refuse to yield; like our own Pennsylvania Plain People who have fought, and continue to fight for the principles they believe in.' His lips brushed her temple, his breath tickled her ear. 'What principle are *you* fighting for, my sweet? What belief?'

My belief in love. The disclosure longed to be exposed. Brandy moved her head slowly from side to side.

Not to this man. Not now. Probably not ever. Even while maintaining a liaison with one woman he proposes to another. No, this was the last man to speak of love to.

'Accept my offer, Brandy,' he whispered cajolingly. 'We both have pride—perhaps too much. We're both strong. We're both fierce fighters. Together we'll be magnificent.' His lips hovered over her ear. His voice was barely discernible. 'We'll produce some fantastic young.'

Brandy gulped back the sob that tore at her throat. She wanted the right to bear those fantastic young. *His* young.

In that moment she realised she would endure anything to acquire that right. In the end she knew she would yield. Not tonight, not tomorrow, but very, very soon.

She could withstand the challenge of a sensual assault. She could even withstand Mitch's cajoling blandishments. She could *not* withstand his tenderness, or the promise of mothering his progeny.

'Are you falling asleep?' Laughter enriched the tenderness of his tone.

Brandy rubbed her forehead against his chest in answer, burrowing closer to his warmth. She wasn't falling asleep but, held like this, she very easily could. What will it be like, she wondered, to sleep the night through in his embrace? The mere thought caused an anticipatory shiver.

Mitch misread the shiver as fatigue. 'It's been a long day, and an eventful night. You're exhausted.' His lips blazed a trail from her ear to the corner of her mouth. 'I won't say I don't want to spend the night with you, because I do. Tonight, tomorrow, and tomorrow night, for that matter, just for starters.' His teeth nibbled her lower lip, increasing the shiver to a full shake. 'I'm pretty desperate to have you, Brandy.'

His urgency, combined with his tenderness, was nearly her undoing. The intensity of her need to have his teasing mouth take possession of hers alerted her to how very close she was to complying with his plea to— give it up.

Bringing her hands up to his chest, she pushed, gently, while taking a step back.

'I'm tired, Mitch,' she sighed. 'And I have a busy day tomorrow, with several special orders to fill. I—I——'

'I know.' Dropping his arms, he stood still, his eyes studying her face, her drooping shoulders. 'You want me out of here so you can go to bed—alone. Right?' A slight smile curved his lips when she nodded mutely. 'I'll go quietly—on one condition.'

'And that is?' Brandy eyed him warily.

'You agree to have dinner with me tomorrow night.' His tone warned that he'd brook no argument.

'All right.' Although Brandy sighed her agreement, a warm glow filled her body.

CHAPTER NINE

BRANDY had not been prevaricating to hasten Mitch on his way when she claimed a full day Saturday.

The first order of business was to call her grandmother's home and tell her sisters the obscene caller had been caught. Her own spirits were buoyed by the girls' relieved and delighted reaction to the news, and with a light step, Brandy carried her second cup of coffee into her workroom.

Working swiftly, competently, she soon dispatched the first three of her special orders, which were all wedding candles. After embedding the parchment wedding invitations into eight-inch pillars, she coated the outside of the candles with a whipped, frothy wax, which she then trimmed with gold to frame the invitations.

When she finished she stepped back to examine the completed work critically. Her glance licked over the white and gold cylinders, then came to rest on the embossed script on the invitations. The lettering blurred, and in her mind's eye the names of the unknown man and woman changed to read:

Brandy Dianne Styer
To
Mitchell Paul Waring

Shaking her head, Brandy blinked her eyes to dispel the illusion, ruefully acknowledging that her mind had stored the then seemingly unimportant fact of his middle name when Darcy had casually mentioned it weeks ago.

Had her subconscious known, even then, that this was the man she wanted to spend the rest of her life with? she wondered sadly. For, no matter how she fought against it, she knew this *was* the man; the only man.

The memory of the minutes she had spent in his arms the night before filled her mind, heating her body. She had felt the power of him then, the depths of his need. She had also tasted the hunger of her own needs.

A self-derisive smile twisted Brandy's soft, vulnerable lips. She had lashed out at Mitch scornfully for his lust, yet her own was as great.

No! No! Brandy's head moved distractedly from side to side. It's more than that, she defended herself to herself, so very much more. She wanted to grasp greedily at all the financial, emotional, and physical support he had offered her. She wanted to take him up on his proposal and, in a sense, hang on to him as if her very existence depended on him. More shattering still; she wanted to give, give, give any and everything he might ask of her.

You'd be no more than a substitute, the voice of self-preservation came to intrude on her dream of fulfilment. He loves another; one who, for some unknown reason, he cannot have. Perhaps the stunning Donna's personal moral code forbade the assuagement of his physical appetite. Are you prepared to play stand-in? the voice persisted. Will you be able to bear sharing the ultimate intimacies with him knowing he is thinking of another woman?

'Oh!'

Brandy's soft outcry of pain was caused by her teeth digging into her trembling lower lip. The cry was followed by a soft, protesting moan. 'But she's not free, and I am, and I love him!'

Brandy was not going to heed the cautioning voice, and she knew it. If there was pain and disillusion in store for her down future's road, she would, somehow, deal with it when she reached it. For now, her decision had been made; she was going to accept Mitchell Waring as husband, as lover, as protector.

In total self-honesty, Brandy admitted that there was no other way for her to go. She needed his emotional support. She needed *him*! For, even now, a whole night removed from the moments she had spent in his overtly suggestive embrace, Brandy's body burned with that need.

The mere thought of experiencing the fullness of his possession sent a chill to coat her inner heat, oddly inflaming her even more. Brandy was not ignorant of a man's lovemaking. In fact, in the case of Charles, one particular encounter had become quite heated. Yet, incredibly, at the age of twenty-six she was still, technically, a virgin.

Always, at the last moment, she had withdrawn from the final commitment of her body to another. In witnessing Charles' frustrated discomfiture, she had been filled with self-disgust at her own careless handling of his emotions, yet she could not take that final step.

In the end it had been her inability to give freely of herself that had caused their parting, not her family responsibilities. Now, Brandy shuddered at the memory of Charles' last bitter words to her.

'You're not a woman at all,' he'd accused harshly. 'You're the worst kind of a tease. God! To think I was considering asking you to marry me! Some marriage that would be ... with a frigid half-woman in my

bed!' His eyes had swept her body with a coldness he
had never displayed before. 'Goodbye, Brandy. I
won't say it's been fun,' he jibed, 'because it sure as
hell hasn't been!'

Brandy had watched him walk away from her, too
stunned to call after him, or even move.

A shudder rippled through her again, and she shook
her head to dispel the ringing echo of his stinging
indictment. Was she a tease? A half-woman? Frigid?

The steady flame, still licking at her being, denied
the accusation. The flame seemed to assure her that
there was one man who could, with very little effort,
draw her into the maelstrom of complete sensuous-
ness.

A shiver of a different type zig-zagged down her
spine.

'Yes, Yes.' Brandy was unaware she had whispered
the acceptance of her fate aloud, for at that instant she
was lost to reality in a fantasy of the lure of Mitchell
Waring's arms.

The gentle clarion of the tiny bells mounted on the
inside of the red door called her back to the here and
now.

For two hours her customers came like grapes—in
bunches. Sales were satisfyingly brisk and when the
last customer departed she went back to her workroom
with a lightened step.

She worked carefully and skilfully on the last of her
special orders; a rose candle nestled in a fragile, long-
stemmed wine glass her customer had provided.

Fashioning each petal of the rose separately from
softened lilac-tinted wax discs, her clever hands
created a blossom that was almost the equal of nature's
own.

To Brandy's disappointment the morning's influx of

customers had not been a harbinger of renewed business activity. Except for the four women who dashed into the shop, gushing thanks for her swiftness and artistry in the execution of their special orders, and a few 'merely lookings', the day dragged on unprofitably.

It was a relief from utter boredom when the phone rang half an hour before closing time.

'Candleglow,' Brandy answered pleasantly. 'May I help you?'

'In many, many ways.' The low, suggestive tone stole all the strength from her legs and, gripping the receiver, Brandy sank on to the high stool she kept behind her counter near the phone. She found the strength had also deserted her vocal cords, for the sound that passed her lips was little more than a whisper.

'Mitch.'

'Yes, little girl,' he whispered back. Then he sent all her strength scurrying by asking, still in a whisper, 'Are you going to marry me?'

Her decision had been made early that morning. Now Brandy acted, if weakly, on it.

'Yes, tall man.'

Silence. Silence that drew out each second to infinity and clawed at her nervous system. Then, barely discernible, but there, whispering along the wire, a sigh.

'Good.'

That one, so satisfied-sounding word had the subtlety of a sledgehammer; it pounded her entire being into mushy submission. God, she loved him! And that one, so softly spoken word had conveyed to her how much he wanted her. That would be enough for her. She would make it enough. She *had* to.

'Brandy?'

'Yes, Mitch.'

'I promise, you won't be sorry,' Mitch vowed in an oddly rough tone. 'I'll make it—all of it—as easy for you as I can.'

Brandy did not miss the inflection, or the deeper meaning in his promise. He believed she was afraid of him. Afraid not only of his overwhelming size, but of his strength, his dominating personality, his take-over attitude.

He was absolutely correct in his belief. She *was* afraid of all those things. She had run her own show, shouldered her own responsibilities, done her own thing too long to meekly hand her life's reins over to him without a qualm. They would clash, often, she knew that too. She also had a sneaky suspicion that she would emerge the loser in those clashes. The fear of him, or her own suspicions, was not strong enough to deter her. She loved him. End of self-argument.

'Did you hear me?' Surely the note that laced his tone could not be anxiety? Brandy shrugged the ludicrous notion aside—of course not!

'Yes.'

'Do you—fully understand?'

'Yes.'

'Your answer is the same?'

This time Brandy imagined a breathlessness in his tone. Don't be naïve, she chided herself.

'Yes.'

'Okay.' Brisk now, decisive, Mitch was suddenly all business. 'We'll make plans over dinner. What time do you close the shop today?'

Brandy glanced at the wall clock that now read: four-forty-two.

'In exactly eighteen minutes.'

'Good.' This 'good' had a different intonation altogether. 'I missed lunch and I'm starving. Can you be ready by six?'

'Of course,' Brandy replied with false indifference, set back by his sudden brusqueness.

'What's the matter?' Mitch didn't miss the inflection either. 'Am I moving too fast for you?'

He was, but Brandy wasn't going to admit it.

'You're too big to be that agile,' she retorted smoothly.

'You think so?' Mitch almost purred. 'You have yet to see me in action, sweetheart. I've got some moves to show you that will not only blow your fuses, but your entire circuit and mind as well.'

'Oh, my heavens!' Brandy managed to sound dutifully flustered. Then, coolly, deliberately she repeated her taunt to her caller of the night before. 'Promises, promises.'

'When!' Mitch whooshed exaggeratedly. 'For a minute there I was worried you were thoroughly cowed.' He paused, then sank his own taunt. 'And I was so looking forward to taking you.'

'You want a tame lapdog in your home?' she asked sweetly.

'No,' he crooned softly. 'What I want is a hellion in my bed.' His full, exciting laughter erupted at her startled 'Oh!' and through it she heard him repeat:

'I'm starving. See you at six.'

As she had known it would, the doorbell chimed on the dot of six. Ready, and waiting for the peal, Brandy opened the door before the ringing echo had ceased.

Looking enormous, and far too attractive from his crisp dark hair to his buffed wing-tips, Mitch stood, easily relaxed, his hazel eyes alight with appreciation and amusement.

'Are you normally prompt, I wonder?' he drawled teasingly. 'Or dare I hope you were eager to see me?'

'Actually, I missed lunch too.' Picking up on his playful mood, Brandy tilted her head back to smile sweetly up at him. 'My stomach's beginning to get the notion that my throat's been cut. That, and the promise of a free meal, spurred me on.'

His face serious, Mitch lifted one hand to trace a long index finger across her throat. 'You conjure up a grisly picture.' The caressing finger was joined by a very broad hand as he bent his long frame over her. 'The only thing I'll allow slicing across your soft skin is my tongue.'

'Mitch, on the front step!' Brandy gasped as, suiting action to words he slid the tip of his tongue along the line his finger had traced.

'On the front step.' The movement of his lips on her skin ignited tiny sparks. 'On the front pavement.' Brandy shivered as his mouth blazed a fiery trail to her ear. 'In the centre of the square downtown.' His teeth nipped at her lobe, to be rewarded by a low moaning sigh from her trembling lips. 'God, I want you!' His big hands circled her waist to draw her to him.

'Mitch, please stop!' Feeling her resistance, and her bones, melting, Brandy brought her hands up to push against his rock-solid chest. 'Are you trying to scandalise the neighbours?'

'No.' His tongue explored the edge of her ear, his chucklingly expelled breath filled the cavity when she gave an unwilling gasp of pleasure. 'I'm trying to lure you back into the house and into your bed.'

'But I'm hungry!' Brandy protested unwisely.

'Oh, so am I,' he assured her deeply. 'Very, very hungry.'

'For food, Mitchell,' she reproached, pressing more firmly against him.

'Oh, all right,' he sighed exaggeratedly, releasing his hold on her waist. As he straightened, he ran an assessing glance over her face, one dark brow arching rakishly. 'Maybe if I feed you, you'll be less inclined to argue.'

'Don't bet your stores on it,' Brandy retorted with a toss of her curly head as she sailed by him and down the three porch steps.

The gleaming Lincoln was parked at the kerb directly in front of the shop, and as she crossed the pavement to it Brandy examined its classic lines appreciatively. In the half light of the dying day, she could see the vehicle's colour was a deep metallic maroon and not the black she had assumed the night before.

'This thing looks like it'll pass anything on the road but a gas station,' she observed dryly when Mitch reached around her to open the passenger side door. 'Aren't you aware of the energy crunch?'

'Yes, I'm aware of the energy crunch,' Mitch mimicked mockingly. 'I'm also painfully aware of the physical crunch—mine, when I try to stuff my body into a compact car!'

The door thumped closed beside her, and Brandy could not resist smoothing her hand over the crushy leather upholstery as she waited for him to circle around the car and climb behind the wheel.

'Status had nothing to do with your decision of purchase?' she queried, in an overly polite tone.

'Status?' His soft laughter derided her question while it made mincemeat of her bones. 'I don't have to make any statements to the world, or prove anything to myself.' His grin was disgustingly self-confident. 'I know exactly who I am, what I am and where I'm going.' He shook his head in gentle rebuke. 'No, little girl, status had nothing to do with my "decision of purchase". Like many American males, I *like* big cars.' Now his grin was pure devil. 'Isn't it nice that not only can I afford to own it, I can afford to feed it as well?'

Longing to wipe the smugness from his tone, Brandy angled an arch look at him as he inserted the key into the ignition.

'Yes, for now—but what about after you've taken on a wife and ready-made family, one of which will be going to college in the fall?'

His fingers still on the key, Mitch paused to slice a thoughtful glance over her. 'I think my income can bear the strain,' he replied in an ominously quiet tone. 'What are you trying to do, Brandy, give me an opportunity to slip off the hook—or wiggle off it yourself?'

'No, of course not! I was——' Brandy came to a breathless halt, the protest dying on her lips at his suddenly rock-hard expression. Had she, subconsciously, been attempting to withdraw from her hasty decision? As she could not give an unqualified no to her own questions, Brandy shook her head slowly in confusion.

'Does that head motion have a meaning?' Mitch's tone was every bit as hard as his expression.

'Mitch, I—I don't think——'

'Don't say it, Brandy,' he cut her off sharply. 'If you value your lovely slim neck at all, don't say it.' Releasing the ignition key, he lifted his large hand to her throat, long fingers curling around it menacingly, if gently. 'I have no intention of letting you beg off. I told you I want you and, if I want something badly enough, I always get what I want.'

An icy finger of very real fear drew a line down

Brandy's spine. His hold on her throat was light, almost caressing, yet she had the panicky feeling that all the air was being squeezed from her body. What in God's name was she letting herself in for here?

'M—Mitch, please, you—you're frightening me,' she stammered hoarsely.

His long fingers curved around the back of her neck to draw her to him as he lowered his head. 'Then don't anger me, little girl,' he warned softly. 'You said "yes", very clearly and very distinctly. I am going to hold you to it. Do you understand?'

Unable to push a sound through her fear-parched throat, Brandy nodded mutely. Was she out of her mind? she thought wildly. She had known instinctively on first sight of him that he was arrogant and domineering. Now she knew he was dangerous as well! If he had lost his temper, shouted at her, she could have handled it. However, this deadly calm, this subtly implied threat of violence demoralised her completely. What *had* she let herself in for here?

'Part your lips for me, Brandy,' he commanded softly.

Actually afraid now, she obeyed him at once. His mouth touched hers gently, almost tentatively, the movement of his lips a tender inducement. His fingers stroked her nape, creating a tingle that quivered the length of her body.

Dear lord! Oh, dear lord, this was insane! Even with her mind in a state of terror, her body responded to the lure of him like an inferno raging out of control.

The pressure of his mouth increased, and with a strangled sob Brandy twined her arms around his neck, urging him closer.

Her response seemed to sever something within him and, with a growl-like sound rattling in his throat he enclosed her in an embrace that crushed her to the hardness of him from his bruising mouth to his muscle-tautened thighs.

For long moments she was lost to everything but her own suddenly searing need. Moaning softly, she felt herself being forced back and down, on to the supple leather of the car seat. His mouth left hers to brand her cheek, the side of her throat. Muttering imprecations against the lack of space, he covered her smaller frame with his large one like a smothering blanket.

Suddenly unable to move, or even breathe properly, Brandy felt renewed panic quench the flame of desire. Beginning to struggle, she grasped his hair to tug his head away. Her action backfired. Instead of dousing his ardour, it seemed to arouse him to a fever pitch. His teeth nipped painfully at her earlobe, the hard tip of his tongue lanced into her ear.

'Don't deny me, darling,' his hoarse voice partially ordered, partially begged. 'You have to be aware of what you're doing to me.' If she hadn't been, the suggestive movement of his body removed all doubt. 'I must have you!'

Shock froze Brandy beneath him. Did he mean to take her here? On the front seat of his car? In full view of the world in general, and her neighbours in particular?

No! The word of rejection screamed through her mind and out through her lips.

'No! Mitchell, you must stop this! Have you gone mad?' The echo of her shrill voice ricocheted inside the confines of the car. 'Think where we are!'

She had no idea whether it was the shrillness of her voice or the content of her words that penetrated the haze of passion clouding his mind, nor did she care.

She only knew that something had touched his reason, for, grinding out a shocking curse, he pulled away from her, lifting her to a sitting position as he did so.

His actions betraying the effort he was exerting to corral his emotions, Mitch flung himself to the far end of the seat, big hands grasping the steering wheel till his broad knuckles turned white with tension. Breathing deeply, he stared broodingly through the windshield for long seconds before, with a sigh, he turned to face her.

'I'm sorry, Brandy.' His darkened eyes gazed piercingly into hers. 'I have never, ever lost control like that before.' Dragging his left hand from the wheel, he raked it through his dark hair and down the back of his neck. 'I—deliberately frightened you, then came very damned close to compounding my stupidity by committing rape.'

'Mitch, no!' The denial sprang to her lips unbidden from a reasoning faculty that refused to believe he would have committed the offence.

'Yes!' he contradicted sharply. 'Yes,' he insisted, softly this time. 'For a few blind moments there, I was driven by the urge for gratification.' He scowled fiercely, causing her to shrink back against the door. 'Brandy, don't,' he groaned. 'You don't really believe that I'd hurt you, do you?'

'I thought not, but for a second there, you looked so—so——' Brandy faltered at the look of contrition that passed in a spasm over his face.

'I give you my word that nothing like this will ever happen again.' He held his right hand out to her, palm up. Brandy hesitated, then placed her much smaller hand in his. 'Will you trust me, little girl?'

In her mind she heard his impassioned voice of a few minutes ago calling her darling. Of course, he'd been in the throes of a consuming physical drive then. Would she ever hear the endearment from his lips again? Her sigh was unknowingly wistful.

'Maybe I'm the one who's mad,' she smiled tremulously. 'But I think I'd trust you with my life.'

'Thank you.'

Brandy felt the shudder that shook him through the palm of her hand. What manner of a man was this? she wondered. He was so very strong, so sublimely self-confident, yet the confirmation of her trust could set him trembling. Strange, confusing man!

'You're welcome,' she murmured, then in an attempt to lighten the atmosphere, she teased, 'I had thought you were planning to buy me dinner, not have me for it!'

Her attempt was rewarded by a crooked grin. Mitch gave her hand a quick, reassuring squeeze, then reached again for the ignition key, this time to give it a twist to fire the engine.

During the short drive to the restaurant where Mitch had made reservations for them, Brandy took the opportunity to straighten her clothes, restore order to her mass of loose curls, and tax herself on her unquestioning trust in him.

After what had transpired, she had every reason to distrust him, yet she did not. Why? To simply claim love for him as an excuse was not nearly enough. Many women *loved*, and with a lot less reason. So then why had she placed her trust in him? Instinct? Well, maybe, but instinct seemed a bit flimsy as a reason. Woman's intuition? Flimsier still.

In the final analysis, Brandy had to admit she had no concrete reason for her trust. Perhaps the lack of reasons should have bothered her, but oddly it did not. When Mitch drove the car on to the restaurant parking lot Brandy sighed with relief, glad her self-examination was, by necessity, at an end.

The inside of the dining room was dimly lit, the décor was unpretentious; the food was only good enough for heads of state.

In an even more dimly lit far corner of the intimate room, Brandy sat across a small table from Mitch and figuratively wallowed in out-of-this-world cuisine. Conversation was minimal and very surface as they savoured their meal. Becoming more relaxed and mellow as the meal progressed, Brandy's dreamboat was rocked when Mitch delivered his first broadside with the dessert.

'I thought we'd get married next Saturday,' he declared blandly.

'Next Saturday?' Brandy nearly choked on her cheesecake. 'Now I know you're mad! I can't get married next Saturday!'

'Why not?' he enquired, one eyebrow arching as if in extreme surprise.

'Why?' Brandy yelped, though softly. 'Why, because one week isn't nearly enough time!' Her eyes narrowed on his complacent face. 'Why next Saturday in particular?'

'Why, so we can share a room when we go to Williamsburg,' Mitch explained patiently.

'Williamsburg? Williamsburg?' Brandy was beginning to feel like an echo. 'Who's going to Williamsburg?'

'We are.'

'We who?' Ungrammatical, but to the point.

'All of us,' Mitch smiled. 'Darcy, Karen, Bev, you and I. The arrangements are all made.'

'Hold it!' Brandy ordered. 'Stop right there. Now back it up and run it by me again—slowly.'

'I said I've made arran——'

'Wait!' She held up her hand like a traffic cop. 'You didn't back up far enough.' A frown crinkled the smooth skin of her forehead. 'Why Williamsburg, anyway?' In truth she was sure she knew why; she wanted his confirmation of that truth.

'Last weekend, Darcy mentioned——' That was as far as she would let him go.

'Aha!' Brandy again interrupted. 'Darcy! I knew it!'

'If you knew it,' Mitch drawled, 'why did you ask?'

'Continue.' Brandy wasn't about to play teasing word games at this point. Thoroughly annoyed, her challenging stare backed up her order.

'As I was—trying to say,' his eyes mocked her annoyance, 'last weekend Darcy mentioned her longing to see Williamsburg.' His eyebrows shot up. 'She *is* going to major in American history in college, isn't she?'

Brandy nodded once.

'I spent odd moments during the week mulling over a way to get you to allow me to treat her to a few days there while she's on Easter vacation.'

'But you just said "all of us",' Brandy reminded him.

'I know,' Mitch concurred. 'If you'll let me finish?'

'Oh, I wish you would,' Brandy jibed, drawing an appreciative smile from him.

'I had not figured out a way around you yet'—his smile broadened into a grin—'until you said "yes" this afternoon.'

'But that was less than five hours ago!' she exclaimed.

'How long does it take to make a phone call?' Mitch retorted. 'Even all the way to Virginia?'

'Mitchell Waring!' she cried, astonished. 'Are you

telling me you had the gall to make reservations
without consulting me?'

'Yep.'

'Of all the arrogant, overbearing, unmitigated
nerve!' Brandy flung the accusation at him like a
verbal stone.

'Yep.'

'You—you——' Lost for words, she glared at him.

'Calm yourself, little girl,' Mitch advised, his lips
twitching suspiciously. 'What difference does it make,
anyway?' he asked reasonably. 'Unless, of course, you
wanted a big, splashy wedding, with all the craziness
that goes with it.'

'No,' Brandy admitted honestly, 'I didn't, but——'

'But what? You did say yes, didn't you?'

'You know I did.'

'Damn right, I know.' He smiled with self-derision.
'And I gave you ample proof earlier of exactly how
eager I am. So'—he shrugged—'we get married on
Saturday, and on Tuesday we leave, as a family, for
Williamsburg.'

'Tuesday?' Brandy probed.

'Tuesday,' he repeated firmly. 'I want to have you
to myself at least a few days before I take on the role of
surrogate father, or brother, or what have you.' He
paused to let his words sink in before asking, 'Okay?'

What could she say? Oh, she *knew* she could say—
no, wait—it's too soon, but she really didn't want to
say any of those things. She loved him. She *wanted* to
be his wife—the sooner the better. Again she played
the echo.

'Okay.'

The smile that transformed his face held more than
a trace of triumph. What saved him from the sharp
edge of her tongue was that it also held relief, and

pleasure, and some other, vaguely recognised emotion Brandy could not quite define. In confusion, she lowered her eyes to her forgotten dessert and now cold coffee.

'My parents want to meet you and the girls.' Mitch fired his second broadside.

That statement brought her eyes up in a hurry. 'They know about us?' Her dreamboat was beginning to list badly.

'Yes,' he nodded. 'They also know we're getting married on Saturday.'

'I don't believe this,' Brandy breathed, shaking her head dazedly. 'Who else did you tell? Did you place a notice in the paper?'

'No.' Mitch's eyes glowed with amusement. 'I've told no one else. I thought we'd tell the girls together tomorrow. Agreed?'

'Why not?' Brandy shrugged in defeat.

'Well then,' his voice went low, 'since you're in such an agreeable mood,' he hesitated, then went on more softly, 'would you agree to not using any form of protection from the outset?'

Brandy frowned her question at him.

'My mother is sixty years old. She told me to tell you she'd like a grandchild as soon as we could possibly swing it.'

CHAPTER TEN

'Now, by the power vested in me by the State of Pennsylvania, I pronounce you man and wife.'

Thus culminated the most frantic week Brandy had ever lived through.

She didn't know whether to laugh or cry! Actually, she didn't have to do either. Her sisters were laughing for her. Mitch's mother, Edith Waring, and Missi were crying.

Observing Missi as she carefully dabbed at her mascaraed eyes, Brandy recalled their telephone conversation the previous Monday. After the usual greeting was dispensed with, Brandy boldly blurted her news.

'Missi, I'm getting married on Saturday and I'd like you to come,' she'd rushed breathlessly.

'Getting married?' Missi had repeated blankly. 'To whom?' Then, before Brandy could answer, she'd yelped, '*This* Saturday?'

'Yes, I'm——'

'Brandy Styer!' Missi had interrupted in a shout, 'if you don't tell me the man's name this instant, I swear I'll——'

'Mitch Waring,' Brandy inserted the name, then held her breath for the explosion she knew was coming. Missi didn't disappoint her.

'Mitchell Waring?' Missi screamed.

'Yes.'

'But what about Donna?' Missi demanded, then on an indrawn breath, 'Oh, God, Brandy, I'm sorry. Me and my big mouth!'

'It's—It's all right, Missi. I——' Brandy bit her lip. 'I don't know about Donna. Her name has never been mentioned.'

'Oh, Brandy!' Missi moaned. 'The affair has been going on for months, it began within weeks of the break-up of her marriage. Everyone knows that they——'

'I love him, Missi,' Brandy whispered across Missi's good intentions. There was silence for several long seconds before Missi sighed.

'I hope you know what you're doing, Brandy,' Missi's voice betrayed her concern. 'You're my best friend, and I don't want to see you hurt, but I'm very much afraid you're going to be.'

Brandy was very much afraid of the same thing, but she wasn't going to admit it to anyone—least of all Missi.

Shifting her glance, Brandy let her gaze rest on the beaming faces of her sisters, now turned adoringly up to their new brother-in-law. Their reaction had been the complete opposite of Missi's.

For all of Mitch's teasing before dinner early Saturday evening, he had not even hinted at the possibility of spending the night with her when he had delivered her back to her home. His goodnight kiss had been so chaste Brandy convinced herself that, having got his way, Mitch was content to bide his time. He had then taken his leave, promising to return Sunday before the girls came home from their visit to the grandparents.

Although she had been certain she would not sleep at all, Brandy had fallen asleep seconds after slipping between the sheets. She was fully dressed, sipping a mid-morning cup of coffee, when Mitch made his appearance, looking big and heart-meltingly attractive in close-fitting tan brushed denims and a finely knit chocolate brown pullover. At the sight of him Brandy had been thankful for the urge that had guided her own selection of a soft, dove-grey wool skirt and a summer sky blue sweater that enhanced her gently rounded figure.

The coffee she poured for him was still steaming when her sisters burst through the kitchen door. For several minutes mass confusion reigned as all three of the girls insisted on talking at the same time. Finally, Mitch's commanding voice cut through the din; the content of his announcement brought instant, if momentary silence.

'If you magpies will pipe down for a second, I have something to say,' his sharp tone sliced through their babbling. 'That's better. Now, brace yourselves,' he advised, a teasing grin tugging at his lips. 'Your sister and I are getting married this coming Saturday.'

'Fan-tas-tic!' This from an exuberant Bev.

'You're putting us on!' cried an incredulous Karen.

'Really and truly?' begged a hopeful-faced Darcy.

'Really and truly,' Mitch gently assured the seventeen-year-old. 'Do you approve?' Eyebrows arched, his glance swept to the other two girls.

'You bet!' Bev nodded.

'Oh, yes,' Karen sighed.

'Wholeheartedly,' Darcy stated.

'Good.' The hovering grin took control of his lips and his hard white teeth flashed. 'So, let's get this show on the road. We have a lot to do this week.'

Talk about understatement! As soon as the girls had stashed their weekend cases in their respective rooms Mitch hustled them all out of the back door and into the elegant Lincoln, parrying their excited questions about their destination with a maddeningly noncommittal,

'You'll see.'

What they saw, and gasped at, when he had driven the big car out of the city, into the suburbs, was a large natural wood and glass tri-level sitting on a gently sloping knoll that afforded a panoramic view of the surrounding countryside.

Uneasily positive that the house belonged to Mitch's parents, Brandy barely had time to become nervous when he brought the car to a stop in front of the double garage at the end of the macadam driveway and pulled on the handbrake.

'Home!' he announced.

Home?

'Home?' Three young voices from the back seat echoed Brandy's confused thought.

'Right.' Mitch's eyes met Brandy's awakened, challenging stare with hard implacability. 'Everybody out for the guided tour.'

'Mitch——' Brandy began.

'Later.' His tone brooked no arguments.

As it turned out, there was no argument later, for Brandy stepped inside the house and fell in love with it.

The floor at ground level contained a large family room, a laundry room, and an enclosed area that housed the heating and air-conditioning units. The second and largest level consisted of a roomy, fully equipped kitchen, a good-sized dining area, a large, airy living room, three bedrooms, two full bathrooms, and a powder room. The third level contained just three rooms; a large bedroom, connecting bathroom, and a walk-in closet storage room.

They began their tour at ground level and when

they reached the bedrooms on the main floor, Mitch grinned at the girls and waved his hand encompassingly.

'I guess you three girls will have to flip a coin to see who gets which room. Don't let the lack of furniture upset you; we'll go shopping after we get back from Williamsburg.'

'Mitch, that's not necessary!' Brandy had protested through the gleeful whoops of her sisters.

'I know,' he replied complacently with a light shrug. 'I want to do it. The master bedroom is furnished,' he continued, 'but you may change anything that doesn't suit you.'

The large master bedroom's décor was quite masculine, almost spartan. Brandy was in the room not two full minutes before she was visualising different draperies and, perhaps, matching easy chairs by the long, wide windows that took up nearly all of one wall. It was when she caught herself redecorating that she knew the house had captured her heart, she *had* to live in it with him.

'If that overgrown son of mine gives you any trouble you just call me; I'll straighten him out.'

Her reverie shattered. Brandy blinked and smiled shyly at her new mother-in-law, a bubble of laughter rising in her throat at the idea of the slender woman 'straightening' the man mountain she had married mere minutes ago.

Brandy had met Edith and Michael Waring less than three hours after being given the grand tour of her future home. Even though Edith was about the same height as Brandy, she was very slender and appeared delicate and fragile between her tall husband and even taller son—who topped his father by a good two inches. It had not taken Brandy long to find that though Edith looked fragile, she handled both her giants with an ease Brandy envied.

Now Brandy let her glance rest on the woman, laughing through her tears as she embraced her son's sisters-in-law in turn. Fortunately, Edith had taken an immediate liking to the girls.

From Edith, Brandy's gaze slid to Mitch, chatting with her beaming-faced grandparents, her breath catching when she found him watching her. Her breath was released jerkily as, his gaze tangling with hers, he crossed the room to her.

'I think the District Justice would appreciate it if we would all vacate her office.' Mitch shot a glance at the large gold watch on his lightly haired wrist. 'As it's now one-twenty, and the room at the hotel is reserved for one-thirty, I suggest we corral this bunch and take off; we'll be late as it is.'

'All—all right,' Brandy murmured around the tightness in her throat. 'I'll collect Missi, my grandparents, and the girls. You take care of your parents and George.' Brandy had met Mitch's best man, George Fry, on arrival at the District Justice office.

The luncheon the hotel staff provided must have been delicious, Brandy decided when it was finished, for everyone said it was. She herself couldn't say, for although she ate some of it she tasted nothing. She wasn't nervous about the coming evening; she was flat out terrified. Try as she would, she couldn't erase the memory of how Mitch had lost control the previous Saturday, and the fear of him doing so again, tonight, had her stomach tied in knots.

It was nearly dinner time before the luncheon party finally broke up, and later still before all the guests had departed to go their separate ways; Darcy, Karen, and Bev still laughing as they assured Mitch they would be packed and ready to leave for Williamsburg at his threatened time of six-thirty Tuesday morning.

'You'd better be,' he warned as Brandy's grand-parents herded them along with them to spend the two intervening days.

Silence permeated the big car as Mitch tooled the Lincoln out of the traffic-clogged city. Growing more tense by the minute, Brandy wondered in amazement at how adroitly he had kept her and her sisters moving during the last week. What with removing all her own personal things from what was her home to what would be her home, helping the girls to decide what to move to the house and what to take along to their grandparents for their trip *and* the days between, shopping for the cream-coloured suit and the accessories to be married in, accompanying Mitch to take care of all the legalities involved, and running the shop, she had barely had time to think, let alone get nervous. Was it possible that Mitch had planned it that way?

Of course! Brandy's spine stiffened against the soft leather seat back. Mitch hadn't wanted her to think, for had she given her rash decision any in-depth consideration, she probably would have bolted the county—possibly the country.

Why had he been in such a hurry? Lowering her lashes, Brandy sliced a glance at him from the corner of her eye. In profile, his expression appeared to her to be of smug satisfaction, as if he'd pulled off a major coup. Why? The answer that presented itself to her now questioning mind made her uneasy.

Had he just procured for himself a front in the guise of a wife? A front that would keep his house and warm his bed? That last thought chilled her blood. Was she totally out of her mind?

Brandy's lashes lowered fully, blocking out his image. What had become of her good sense, her independent spirit? Unbelievably, she was about to lavish her innocence on a man who loved another woman!

Biting down on her lip, she suppressed the shudder that attempted to rip through her body. Dear God, she loved him! She longed to be all things to him. Her teeth dug more deeply into her lip. All he wanted from her was the regular use of her body! She could not even accuse him of being dishonest with her. Mitch had been honest to the point of bluntness. He had a frustration that demanded appeasment; she had just agreed, through the traditional marriage vows, to be the appeasee. No doubt about it whatever, she *was* totally out of her mind!

Brandy's lashes fluttered open at the cessation of motion to find the car at rest in the driveway of her new home. *Her* home? A sob clawed at her throat. She *had* no home! Mitch had contracted to have the entrance to her shop made private, the second and third floors to be remodelled into an apartment. He already had a tenant, ready and waiting to move in! In effect, he had closed off her avenue of retreat.

The full realisation of what she had committed herself to hit her with the force of an actual blow and she had to gulp back a bubble of sick hysteria.

'Are you asleep with your eyes wide open?'

Suppressing yet another shudder, Brandy blinked and refocused her eyes on her husband's strangely taut face. Her husband! Oh God!

'No, of course not. I . . . I . . .' She raked her mind for a plausible reason for staring into nothingness. 'I was just wondering what I was going to do with all the furniture at home.' Even to her own ears the excuse sounded puny.

'*This* is your home.' Impatience was clear in his tone and the movement of his head as he nodded at the tri-level. 'I told you I'd take care of all the stuff you didn't want to bring with you.' His tone rapped, if gently, at her. 'Didn't I?'

'Yes, but . . .'

'Second thoughts, Brandy?' His tone was now so soft it made her uneasy. Before she could form an answer he made one unnecessary. 'If you're having some, forget them. It's too late. You *are* my wife. So, shall we go into our house? Or were you planning to set up housekeeping right here in the car?'

'It's almost big enough.' Brandy hadn't the vaguest idea how she'd managed to dredge up the quip, or the bantering tone, but on that lighter note she got out of the vehicle in question.

'Perhaps.' Mitch's soft laughter followed her along the flagstone path to the steps that led to the redwood deck that surrounded the second level. 'But as a bedroom it leaves a lot to be desired.'

He *would* mention the word bedroom! Brandy clamped her lips against a groan. How was she going to get through the coming hours? Her innocence cried out for gentleness and tenderness, but Mitch was completely ignorant of her innocence. His expectations were of a woman experienced in the ways of assuaging a man's physical appetite. Boy, was he in for a surprise!

In the next instant she concluded that he wasn't the only one in for a surprise as, without even giving her time to remove her coat, he slid his arm around her waist to urge her up the stairs to the master bedroom.

Her mind blank to any delaying tactics, Brandy moved beside him numbly, her memory of his near attack on her the week before filling her with dread.

Her legs carried her into the centre of the large bedroom and then, her eyes frantically shying away from his enormous bed, she came to a dead stop, her legs refusing to take one more step. Mutely, her gaze fastened on the forest green fibres of the carpet, she endured Mitch's touch as he removed her coat and then her suit jacket. Mitch had voiced his appreciation of her wedding attire when she had met him at the District Justice's office. Now he repeated his earlier compliment.

'This is a lovely garment,' he murmured as he dropped the jacket carelessly on to the floor. 'You didn't happen to buy it at one of the Waring stores, did you?'

'N . . . no,' Brandy shook her head, despairing at the croaking sound of her voice. 'I . . . I found it in a little out-of-the-way boutique.'

'Hmmm,' he murmured. 'The blouse is nice too,' he whispered as his fingers slid over the silky material to the small pearl buttons.

A trembling began as the top button slipped through its slot, and grew in volume as his fingers moved down, making quick work of each successive pearl. Brandy was quivering all over by the time the feather-light blouse floated down to join the jacket on the floor. Her smooth, pencil-slim skirt followed moments later.

'Step out of your shoes.'

Brandy's body jerked at the soft command. Her breathing becoming restricted, she obeyed him without demur. His fingers seared her skin everywhere he touched as he divested her of her lacy bra and filmy half slip, then, on her gasp of disbelief, he knelt before her to slowly, carefully smooth her ultra-sheer pantyhose over her hips and down her now shaking legs. Her eyes tightly closed, Brandy felt his movement when he rose to his feet, felt his warm breath feather her naked skin when he half ordered, half pleaded:

'Look at me, Mrs Waring.'

Lifting her lids was one of the hardest things she had ever had to do. When the task was completed she stared, her cheeks growing pink at the incongruity of herself, stark naked, facing a fully clothed husband. His next whispered command set her cheeks to flame.

'Now it's your turn to undress me.'

Oh, sweet heavens, she couldn't do it . . . could she? Raising leaden arms, she ordered her stiff, trembling fingers to loosen his muted gold tie. When the silk neckpiece slithered snake-like to the floor, she directed icy fingers to the buttons on his brown waistcoat. Long seconds later, his waistcoat and jacket covered the tie and, avoiding his eyes, she gritted her teeth and set to work on the buttons of his pristine white silk shirt. By the time the shirt whispered to the carpet, Brandy was finding it very hard to breathe at all. The fact that Mitch's breathing was becoming raspy also seemed to have an odd effect on her pulse rate.

Other than where necessary while removing her clothing, Mitch had not touched her. Now, as her fingers fumbled with his belt buckle, his fingers grasped her around the waist—almost convulsively.

'I can't take much more of this,' he groaned huskily. 'Are you deliberately being so slow in a bid to drive me out of my mind?'

'No!' Brandy gasped. God, the last thing she wanted was to find herself trapped in a bedroom with a mindlessly aroused male! With her protest her eyes flew to his, and she immediately wished she'd kept them lowered. His eyes, darkened to an emerald green, glittered with the desire that gripped his body. At sight of the passion blazing with green fire, Brandy gasped aloud.

'It's there for you to see, isn't it?' Mitch rasped as he very slowly lowered his head to hers. 'The evidence of how very badly I want you is written plainly on my face, isn't it?' he demanded, his lips a half breath away from hers. His hands loosened their hold on her waist and slid down, over her buttocks, drawing her body to his. Contact brought another, sharper gasp to her lips. 'Don't be afraid of me, Brandy,' he murmured soothingly when she stiffened. 'I'm no different from other men.'

That's what I'm afraid of! Brandy protested silently. There have *been* no other men! She had to tell him. She should have told him last week!

'Mitch . . .' That was as far as she got, for his mouth took possession of her parted lips.

His kiss was totally different from the assault he had made on her mouth the week before. It was even different from the way he had kissed her in her kitchen the night they had apprehended their phone abuser. This kiss was a seduction of the mouth, the senses, the mind. Suddenly her body trembled for a different reason.

Heat of a kind she had never experienced roared through her veins to converge throbbingly in the lower part of her body. She was quivering violently when she felt his hands move caressingly down the back of her thighs. Startlingly, the long fingers that stroked her skin trembled almost as violently.

'Brandy, Brandy.'

With the moaning of her name his mouth crushed hers, coaxing hers to join in erotic play. Brandy curled her arms around his strong neck, whimpering with pleasure as her soft breasts stabbed at his hair-roughened chest.

She was lost, and she knew it. When her thighs parted to cradle his thrusting body, Mitch knew it too.

As devastating as it was, the kiss could not suffice, and with a murmured 'wait' Mitch put her from him. Within seconds the remainder of his clothes increased the pile on the floor and sweeping her into his arms he carried her to the bed.

With delicate gentleness and mind-rending slowness, Mitch proceeded to arouse her to a degree she would not have believed possible. Murmuring softly against her heated skin, he urged her to explore him fully. With his hands, and fingers, and warm, moist mouth he brought her to sobbing surrender.

In wonder, she felt her breasts swell to fill his hands and when his lips closed over one hardened bud she cried out in pleasure. For all her earlier fears, in the end it was she who begged to be taken.

'Mitch, please, please, I can't bear any more!'

'There will be more,' he promised as he moved to cover her writhing body with his own. 'The best part starts now.'

His movement was sure and decisive, and instantly stilled when she cried out with the pain of it.

'Brandy . . . what . . .?' he demanded incredulously. Had she had the courage to look at him, she would have seen the mixture of concern and wonder in his expression. As she lacked the courage, she missed it.

'Mitch, I . . . I'm sorry.' She moved her head restlessly on the pillow, eyes tightly closed. 'I know I should have told you but . . . but . . . I'm sorry.'

'Sorry?' In her fear of his displeasure, she also missed the sheer amazement in his tone. 'Sorry? Good God, I'm not.' His lips touched hers gently, enticingly. 'But you should have told me. I would have taken more care.' The play of his tongue, outlining her mouth, caused her breathing to grow shallow again. 'The worst is over now,' he promised. 'Now there's only pleasure.'

Slowly, building shivering tension within them both, he taught her the meaning of physical, ecstatic fulfilment with shattering thoroughness. At the zenith of her desire Brandy shuddered as if in a gale force wind, and gloried in the matching quake that shook her husband's body throughout the entire length of his elongated frame.

The movement of the mattress as Mitch slid back on to the bed beside her roused Brandy out of her satiated doze. Forcing her eyelids apart, she frowned in confusion at the soft glow of light that bathed the room. Sitting up, she blinked and glanced around for the source of that light. A soft gasp whispered through her lips as her gaze came to rest on a candle placed in the centre of the long, gleaming double dresser, its flame flickering evenly, as a well made candle's should.

So that one should, she nodded mentally. Hadn't she made it herself? Her frown grew contemplative. What was that particular, very expensive candle doing here? Hadn't Mitch told her he wanted that candle for a hostess gift? A shiver kissed her skin as one long finger was drawn down her spine.

'It's true what they say about women looking more beautiful by candlelight,' Mitch declared softly. 'Even though I wouldn't have believed you *could* look more beautiful.'

Colour, brought on by his compliment, and the sudden realisation of her nakedness, crept up her neck and over her cheeks. In an attempt to hide her confusion, she took him to task.

'I thought you said you wanted that candle for a hostess gift,' she scolded him softly.

'No,' Mitch denied teasingly, 'I merely said that I needed a hostess gift. Actually, I presented my hostess that evening with a large, exorbitantly priced gold paper-wrapped box of chocolates.' His eyes did a detailed inventory of her from her slim legs to her deeply pinked cheeks. 'I wanted the candle for myself. For tonight.'

'But you couldn't have known!' Brandy gasped.

'No, not then,' he agreed silkily. 'But I did know it would only be burned on a very special occasion.' Languidly, he lifted one long arm to encircle her waist and draw her down on to his chest. 'And you will have to admit that this *is* one very special occasion.'

Brandy could not have denied his assertion had she been so inclined, for his parted lips caught hers, driving all thought out of her mind.

It was not until Monday evening that Brandy realised, with a jolt of shock, that, except to bathe, and consume some hastily prepared meals, she and Mitch had not set foot out of the bedroom.

Had she actually chastised *him* about lust? she asked herself in wonder, as she folded clothes and placed them neatly in her suitcase. Warmth pervaded her body as she remembered how eager she had been to learn all he had to teach her about the art of lovemaking. Mitch had promised her pleasure and he had kept his promise exquisitely. Brandy now knew she no longer loved Mitchell Waring. The emotion that filled her entire being for him now could only be described as near adoration.

Whistling tunelessly, the object of her emotion-packed thoughts sauntered out of the bathroom, into the bedroom, a towel draped around his flat middle, a travel shaving kit in his hands.

'I plan to stop for breakfast tomorrow morning after we make the run around Washington. Okay?' He flipped the shaving kit into his open case, then glanced at her questioningly.

'Yes, of course, you're the driver,' Brandy agreed distractedly, fighting the urge to devour his large frame with her eyes.

'All the way.' The double meaning of his firm statement didn't register until she looked up and saw the laughing light glittering in his passion-darkened eyes.

'Now, Mitchell,' she warned, beginning to back away. 'We have to pack and get a good night's rest. We must get up very early, remember.'

'There is one way of assuring me a good night's rest,' he taunted, stalking her across the room. 'And you know what way that is, don't you, little girl?'

As she turned to run, long arms shot out and caught her, dragging her into a bear-like embrace.

'You've got the appetite of a wild animal,' she accused breathlessly, laughingly.

'And don't you just love it?' he growled into the sensitive skin behind her ear.

Being honest with herself, and him, Brandy whispered 'yes', trembling in expectation as she nipped at his shoulder.

When they collected her sisters at exactly six-thirty Tuesday morning, Brandy was grumpily sleepy and dull as tarnished silver plate. Mitch was disgustingly bright-eyed and alert.

When, finally, the happily chattering trio and their assorted baggage were bundled into car and boot, and

Mitch had turned the car in the direction of Washington D.C., Brandy sighed and let her head loll on the seat's comfortable headrest and promptly fell asleep, not to waken until they stopped for breakfast. The sound of the handbrake being pulled back roused her in time to hear Mitch teasingly ask her not very quiet sisters:

'Is she sleeping, do you think? Or is she stone cold dead?'

'Gee, I hope she's not dead,' Bev replied seriously. 'That would really put a damper on our trip!'

Rested from her nap, her spirits revived, Brandy burst out laughing. 'As you can see, I'm very much alive,' she grinned. 'But I swear, if I don't get something to eat, and quickly, I *will* expire right here in this car!' Her laughing retort set the tone for their entire trip.

They were all beginning to feel uncomfortably numb in the posterior when Mitch followed the curving driveway to the front of the Williamsburg Inn. As the super-efficient staff were expecting them they were graciously and swiftly shown to their rooms in one of the small guesthouses that fronted on to the Duke of Gloucester Street, the main street in the restored area.

The girls were enchanted by the quaint, early American décor of the house and their rooms, but were grateful for the up-to-date concession of air-conditioning and colour TV. They were also in agreement with Mitch's suggestion of a rest before showering and dressing for dinner.

That evening they dined in colonial splendour in the King's Arms Tavern. Served by politely pleasant, costumed waiters, they all opted for the tavern's famous cream of peanut soup, which, they concurred, was well worth every calorie. The soup was followed by oyster pie, corn pudding, sweet potato casserole and Sally Lunn bread. Rich, dark coffee and mouthwatering pecan pie concluded the meal.

'I don't think I'll be able to eat another thing for at least a week,' Karen declared dramatically, as they strolled along the Duke of Gloucester Street after leaving the Inn.

'Or at least until breakfast,' Bev chided before, turning to glance at Mitch, she asked, 'Do we have reservations for breakfast, too?'

'Yes,' Mitch nodded. 'I thought you'd all enjoy brunch at Christiana Campbell's Tavern. I think you'll find it quite an experience.'

'Are we going to have any time at all to do any sightseeing?' Brandy enquired dryly. 'I mean, will there be any time between meals?'

Mitch's soft laughter, blending with the giggles from the three girls walking a few feet ahead of them, floated lightly, pleasantly on the balmy night air. 'One absolutely cannot visit Williamsburg and not sample the food,' he instructed with mock sternness. 'As I plan to dump you all out of the sack very early every morning, we'll have plenty of time to see all the sights.'

Ever true to his word, Mitch did indeed 'dump' them out early the next morning. As the brunch at Campbell's was not served until ten, and they had picked up their necessary tickets at the information centre on their way in the day before, they all eagerly agreed to Mitch's suggestion that they tour the Capitol building before breakfast, as the building was located near Campbell's at the one end of the Duke of Gloucester Street.

The period-costumed guide was charming as well as erudite, and they spent an absorbing hour following her through the rooms that had been reconstructed to match the ones through which so many famous Americans had strode—among them George Washington, Thomas Jefferson, James Madison, and the fiery Patrick Henry, whose compelling portrait on the second floor captured the eye and filled the imagination.

'His eyes hold visions!' Darcy's awe-filled whisper put into words what all of them were feeling.

Brunch was indeed an experience. Chattering animatedly on all she had learned about history in such a short amount of time, Bev paused to giggle when their waiter asked if Brandy and Mitch would care for a cocktail, the idea of a drink before breakfast tickling her funnybone.

Grinning at the irrepressible fourteen-year-old, Mitch ordered a mixture of champagne and Guinness stout called a Black Velvet Cocktail—the very name of which intrigued Bev. The four less intrepid females ordered orange juice. When it came to ordering their food from a mind-boggling selection, they all opted for pecan waffles served with warm maple syrup and sausages.

Replete with breakfast, they ambled back down the Duke of Gloucester Street, the three girls again in the forefront, Brandy and Mitch, arm in arm, bringing up the rear.

'Enjoying yourself?' The question came, very softly, from beside her.

'Yes,' Brandy answered, a little shyly. 'Are you?'

'Hmmm,' Mitch nodded, then, a devilish smile curving his lips, he teased, 'As honeymoons go, this one has got to be the winner!'

Feeling her cheeks growing warm, Brandy lowered her lids, but nodded in agreement. As the girls' room was on the second floor of the guesthouse, and her and Mitch's room was on the first floor, they had complete privacy. The night before, Mitch had taken full advantage of that privacy. Yes, as honeymoons go, Brandy decided dreamily, this one was most definitely a winner. The most amazing thing of all was that Mitch, far from resenting the presence of her sisters, actually seemed to delight in their company. Brandy could not remember ever feeling so content before in her life.

The rest of that day and the two that followed were jammed with sightseeing—and food. Not wanting them to miss anything, Mitch had them moving from early morning till late at night, most times laughing all the way.

Bev was fascinated by the array of bottles and jars—not to mention the container of leeches—in the front room of the apothecary shop, and delightfully horrified by the crude and torturous instruments of 'healing' in the back section.

Karen loved the millinery shop and the display of clothes and materials of the pre-Revolutionary period.

Darcy enjoyed their tour of the Raleigh Tavern, so named for Sir Walter Raleigh. She loftily informed them that Phi Beta Kappa was founded at the Raleigh in 1776, moments before their guide did the same.

Brandy took an avid interest in watching the craftsmen, busy at their various work from binding books to fashioning wooden buckets and barrels, to her own love of candlemaking.

Mitch was amused by the wigmaker's shop, and the costumed young woman who presided over it. As she explained the process of wigmaking, she incorporated several of the men in her audience into her performance, thus making not only wigs, but learning, fun.

It was late afternoon on Friday when they toured the Governor's Palace. Once again the audience was included in the proceedings. Being told they were now a committee there to petition the Governor, they were led through the elegant rooms as such, being informed of the many and various activities that took place there as they went.

After the palace they reverently stepped inside Bruton Parish Episcopal Church to admire the simplicity of design and the practicality of high boxed pews with doors, so built for warmth in the unheated building.

After yet another delicious dinner, this time in Chowning's Tavern, they visited the charming shops in Merchants' Square, which they found located between the foot of the Duke of Gloucester Street and William and Mary College. Although Mitch groaned about being dragged through one store after another, he dipped frequently into his wallet to unstintingly provide the wherewithal for whatever the girls fancied.

Early on Saturday morning they regretfully vacated their rooms to make the short run down the highway to Busch Gardens Old Country. The unique amusement park, laid out in sections representing different countries, was crowded with people. Brandy was delighted with the Beefeater in England. Mitch lingered at the stalls of the big, beautiful Clydesdale horses. Karen liked the German folk dancers in the large beergarden. Darcy enthused over the graceful pillars in the Italian amphitheatre. Bev gorged herself on the food, and thrilled to the rides—the wilder the better—in every country.

They spent the night in a motel not far outside Busch Gardens, then after a leisurely breakfast

Sunday morning, they started for home, the honey-moon over.

It was not until they had made the run around Washington that Brandy was struck with the realisation that she and Mitch had been together one full week, and had not crossed swords once.

CHAPTER ELEVEN

BLADES remained sheathed and, for the entire length of the spring, Brandy lived in a euphoric haze. Throughout that period Mitch revealed facets of his character she would have never dreamed he possessed.

With more patience than even she could have summoned, he helped the girls, each in their turn, to prepare for end-of-term examinations, promising to have an ingrown pool installed if they all passed with a B or better average. With humour and understanding he listened to every one of their trials and tribulations, advising when necessary, nodding sagely when all that was needed was a sympathetic ear. He became all things to the girls that they had lacked for a very long time: brother, uncle, mature male friend.

To Brandy, he simply became all things. Not since her college days had she known such a carefree existence. Almost without her realising he was doing it, he lifted the weight of responsibility from her shoulders and settled it on his own, much broader ones.

In the role of brother, he was very, very good. In the role of husband he was excellent. In the role of lover, he was nothing short of magnificent.

Brandy spent those weeks of spring working in her shop, shopping for her new home, and learning how to please the gentle man-mountain she had married.

She was more than merely happy; she was serenely content. This was her mental condition on a hot

Monday afternoon as she lay on a lounger beside the completed pool, a soft smile on her lips as she listened to her laughing sisters cavorting in the sparkling blue water.

'Phone call for you, Mrs Waring.'

The voice belonged to Emily Wagner, the woman Mitch had hired, against Brandy's wishes, as house-keeper-cook.

'Coming!'

With a sigh, Brandy swung her slim, newly tanned legs off the gaily padded cushion. Picking up a towel, she wiped coconut-scented oil off her hands as she crossed the smooth lawn to the redwood steps.

'Sorry to disturb you,' Emily, holding the door open for Brandy, apologised as she entered the house, 'but he said it was important.'

He? Brandy frowned as she tracked over the carpet in the hanging plant-filled living room to the corner desk, upon which rested the burnt orange-coloured phone.

'Hello?'

'Brandy?'

For a moment Brandy's mind was totally blank, then she put a face to the male voice.

'Yes, Jason.' Why in the world was *he* calling *her*?

'I called to congratulate you.' Jason answered her silent question.

Wasn't it proper to congratulate the groom?

'That was some feat you pulled off.'

Feat? Brandy's frown deepened. Whatever was Jason talking about? Unhappily, he did not leave her dangling in the dark.

'Everybody's been observing the affair between Waring and the luscious Donna for months, and in early spring it became obvious she really had him strung out. Did you catch the bastard in a moment of frustration?'

Brandy couldn't answer, simply because she could barely breathe. She hadn't even been aware that Mitch and Jason knew each other! She knew she had to say something—but what? Again he spared her the effort.

'So you managed to get what you wanted after all,' Jason went on silkily. 'But I'm curious. Did you two strike some kind of a bargain?'

'Bargain?' Brandy's voice croaked through her suddenly raw throat. She had an inkling of what was coming. Sadly her inkling proved correct.

'Yes, of course.' Jason's tone was as smooth as expensive porcelain. 'I know you, remember? I know all about your uptight independence. What was the deal? He gives you the financial backing to continue in your guise of little mother and, in return, you provide him with a front of respectability to hide his amour behind?'

Brandy cringed, inside, outside. The worst was yet to come.

'I just thought I'd call and let you know it's working. But then I knew if anyone could pull it off, you could.' The taunting note in his tone alerted her, giving her time to steel herself.

'I've seen them together several times since the wedding. She no longer looks quite so harried. He no longer looks quite so frustrated. And, most importantly, no one looks at them with quite the same amount of suspicion.'

All the brightness went out of the day, and her life. All the fear she had buried deep down in her consciousness rose to envelop her. It had been *too* good to be true. She had been *too* happy. Using every ounce of control she possessed, Brandy plunged her voice into iciness.

'Goodbye, Jason. And do me a favour, please. Don't ever call me again.'

Moving slowly, she carefully cradled the receiver, then closed her eyes against the crushing pain. A front! How many others beside Jason thought of her as a front? Her lips twisted. Hadn't she thought the same—light years ago?

It's not true! Not Mitch! Not *her* Mitch! The protest swelled to fill her mind, her entire being. Not the Mitch she had come to know these last weeks, never *that* Mitch!

The anguish vanished from her face, to be replaced by determination and decision. She'd prove Jason wrong! Now, at once! Spinning around, Brandy ran up the stairs to the large bedroom she had so blissfully shared with Mitch.

Less than an hour later, having showered and dressed in a new, most becoming sundress and strappy sandals, Brandy parked the new little Escort, that had replaced the battered VW, on a downtown lot and walked with quick, long strides to the Waring shop.

Ignoring the questioning glances sent her way by a few of the clerks, she traversed the length of the store and, forcing herself not to run, mounted the stairs to Mitch's second-floor office.

Donna was not at her desk in the outer office. The door that connected the two rooms was ajar. Crossing the thickly carpeted floor, Brandy nudged the door wider to discover *why* Donna was not at the front desk. It was impossible for her to man the front desk while being enfolded in her employer's arms. The desk was empty. Mitch's arms were not!

Was it possible for the world to stop? Perhaps not, but at that moment, for all intents and purposes, the world stopped for Brandy. Mitchell Waring, *her* husband, was bent protectively over the statuesque Donna, his head resting on her sunlight-bright hair. Donna was crying softly.

Why was she crying? The question flashed through Brandy's mind, followed immediately by the obvious answer: You know damn well why she's crying; legally, he must share his bed with his wife!

Had she gasped aloud? Had she moaned? Brandy didn't know, but something alerted Mitch to her presence. With an unusual clarity of vision she saw his body tense before he lifted his head to stare at her out of eyes opaque with alarm. Donna, feeling him tauten, stirred, then glanced around, her woebegone expression changing to one of horror.

'Oh, no!' she half gasped, half sobbed.

'It's all right,' Mitch's tone soothed, even as he put her from him. 'Go to the rest room and repair your face.' His tender tone, the gentle way he turned and pointed her towards the office's other exit, slashed at Brandy's emotions like razor-sharp claws. Although his eyes didn't leave Brandy's face, he didn't speak until the door clicked shut behind Donna.

'It's not what you think.'

Not a trace of the alarm that had flashed in his eyes at the sight of her tinged the even tenor of his voice. Brandy hadn't the vaguest idea what she had expected from him. Protestations of innocence, perhaps? Or even bravado? Maybe, but she sure hadn't expected a mildly delivered 'It's not what you think'.

Anger flared. How the hell did he know *what* she thought? Had she become so very transparent to him? The thought disturbed her so very badly that, for the first time in weeks, she brought all her defences to the fore. As her barriers rose, her voice lowered.

'Of course not.'

Her reply was not what *he* had expected. Eyelids narrowing, he took a step towards her, then halted when she backed up.

'Brandy, I . . .'

'I don't want to talk about it!' Her tone lowered the temperature by at least ten degrees. Her eyes swept the room disparagingly. 'At least, not here.' She punctuated her statement by turning away from him.

'Brandy, wait! We'll go home to . . .'

That was all she heard, for by then, she was hurrying down the stairs. She was positive he would not cause a scene by rushing after her through the store. She was correct, he did not. Standing on the sidewalk outside the store, Brandy paused, delicate nostrils flaring. What to do? Where to go? She felt sure Mitch would go directly home, expecting to find her there, but she was just not ready to hear whatever he had to say—be it explanation or excuse.

Moving like a sleepwalker, she stared into plate-glass windows with unseeing eyes. Precisely when the rebellion began uncoiling inside, she did not know, but suddenly it flared, full blown.

The Mitchell Waring she had come to know was incapable of this kind of deceit! Cool now, she deliberately let her mind travel back over the weeks since her marriage.

In her mind's eye she pictured Mitch, his arm draped casually around her waist or over her shoulder as they strolled the tree-shaded streets of Colonial Williamsburg, patiently and smilingly answering the seemingly endless stream of questions her sisters put to him.

Mitch, his hand clasping hers as they wended their way through the crowds at Busch Gardens, squeezing her fingers in communication when, on his teasing, negative shake of the head at Bev's query of whether he'd go on the Loch Ness Monster ride with her, he threw back his head and roared with laughter when Bev moaned:

'How can I fly like an eagle when I'm surrounded by a bunch of turkeys?'

Mitch, patiently suffering his bride's redecorating schemes, even to shrugging off several raps on the head from walking into the planters she had hung all over the house.

Most heartwrenching of all, Mitch, his words ardent, his hands enticing, his mouth hot as he led her into a world of exquisitely beautiful physical pleasure that seemed to transcend into the spiritual.

His gentleness, his tenderness, his understanding with her, and her sisters. *This* was the Mitchell Waring she would follow to the heights of heaven or the depths of hell. *Had* this same Mitchell Waring been deceiving her with another woman all these weeks?

Hurt, confused, Brandy racked her brains for an answer. She didn't want to believe what her eyes had witnessed. There could be a very reasonable explanation. Couldn't there?

She came to an abrupt halt. There was only one way to find out, and that was to go home and face it out. Glancing around to get her bearings, Brandy frowned, then strode off in the direction of the lot where she had parked her car.

At least she had covered her most vulnerable flank, she sighed as she unlocked the car Mitch had given her for a wedding present. She had never at any time allowed herself to confess her love for him. The words had trembled on her lips countless times, yet she had held them back, waiting, praying to hear the vow pass his lips first.

Driving towards home and the inevitable confrontation, Brandy breathed a thankful prayer that she had kept silent. She was feeling deep pain now, had she given him the opportunity to throw her love back in her face, she wasn't sure she could bear it.

On entering the house Brandy was struck by the realisation that it was strangely quiet. Where were the girls? Where was Mrs Wagner? Most pressing of all, where was —Mitch? His car was in the driveway, so—It was really quite impossible to overlook a man of his size!

'What took you so long?' Brandy jumped, startled, as his voice preceded him into the living room from the stairway to the ground level. 'Did you take the scenic route?'

She had been wandering around in a blue funk, tearing herself to shreds over him—and he was being droll? Anger nearly choking her, Brandy spun to face him, her eyes spitting fire. In her agitation, she didn't notice his lack of colour, or the tightly controlled line of his lips.

'Where are the girls and Emily?' she demanded. 'Did you send them away to spare them my hysterics?'

'Are you planning to become hysterical?'

Had his voice held a hopeful note? Brandy dismissed the very idea. There wasn't a man breathing who *hoped* his wife was going to become hysterical. 'Are you planning to continue this office hours liaison?' she shot back coldly.

'Dammit, Brandy, there is no liaison, not during or after office hours.' His body taut, he came to tower over her. 'And I paid Emily to take the girls out to dinner so we could discuss this in private.' He stepped still closer, towering even more intimidatingly.

'No liaison?' Refusing to be intimidated, Brandy glared up at him. 'What exactly would you call that little scene I barged in on this afternoon?'

'That little scene was no more than one human offering comfort to another.' Mitch's voice, his entire body were tight.

'How interesting.' Somehow, Brandy had managed a very uninterested tone. 'The way I understand it, these offerings are made quite often.'

'The way you understand it,' Mitch repeated softly, eyes narrowing. 'The way you understand it from whom?'

'Oh, a friend,' Brandy laughed—well, almost. 'Isn't it always, "a friend" who tells the wife, who is *always* the last to know?'

Now she did notice his lack of colour, because he went decidedly grey. A telltale, guilty grey? Brandy wondered sickly.

'What friend?' he asked grimly, if softly.

'What difference does it make?' she cried. 'Is it or is it not true that you and Donna have been seen out together?'

'Probably,' he bit the one word off. 'But, as I told you, it's not what you think.'

'No, of course not.' Now she did back away from him—simply because she was sure that if she did not, she would hit him. 'It's all quite platonic,' she sneered—simply because she was sure that if she did not, she would weep.

'After the nights we've spent together, you really believe I could bed another woman?' Mitch laughed incredulously. 'What do you think I am, super-stud?'

'Don't you dare get cute with me!' she stormed.

'I'm not being cute.' Mitch advanced, and Brandy retreated. 'Whether you know it or not, woman, I've given you every damn thing that's in me.'

'Everything but fidelity.' Unwilling to have him see her cry, Brandy spun away from him. Instantly his big hand grasped her arm to swing her around to face him.

'And you've given me everything but your trust,' Mitch accused bitterly.

'Trust? Trust? What do you know about trust?' Brandy sobbed, unable to stem the tears that sprang to her yes. 'I knew about your affair with Donna before I married you. Yet I *trusted* you to end it at the time of our marriage. Now I know my trust was misplaced.'

'You knew?' He stepped to within a few inches from her. 'You knew, and yet you married me. Why?'

Oh God! How could she have made such a tactical error? More to the point, how could she regroup?

'I—I—you offered me security and—and——'

'No, Brandy.' Mitch's eyes gleamed with the light of sensed victory. 'There's no way in hell you, of all people, would agree to marry a man you suspected of *already* being involved with another woman, merely to attain security.' Lowering his head, he brushed her temple with his lips. 'And you're jealous, have been ever since you walked into my office this afternoon.' His voice held something very like awed excitement. 'You are jealous, aren't you?'

Bending lower, his lips tasted the delicate skin at the corner of her eye, then skimmed down her cheek to the corner of her mouth. 'Why are you jealous?' he demanded in a whisper.

'Let me go, Waring.' Even to her own ears Brandy's order lacked conviction.

'I want an answer.' His teeth nibbled at her lower lip.

'Don't do that, Mitchell!' Brandy despaired at the breathless sound of her voice.

'Why, Brandy?' The hard tip of his tongue drew a shiver from her as it traced the contour of her mouth.

'Please stop, Mitch.' Her groan was barely audible.

'I love you, Brandy.' His mouth crushed her lips. His arms crushed her body to his.

'You don't!' Brandy sobbed when he lifted his head to gaze down at her. 'There's Donna, and——'

'There was *never* Donna. She's a friend, no more. A very unhappy friend who loves her husband, although, for the life of me, I don't know why.' His head dipped again and his mouth ate hers hungrily for long, sanity-shattering moments.

'I love you, Brandy.'

Brandy believed him—she had to, for, suddenly, the man her arms came up to and clasped was not the confident, self-assured man she had known, but a giant trembling in her arms.

'Dear God, Brandy, tell me I'm not wrong. Tell me why you were so angry and jealous.'

'You ox,' she chided softly. 'You big, darling ox. Yes, I was jealous. When I saw you holding her in your arms, I wanted to kill you. I wanted to kill her!' Her arms tightened possessively. 'Oh God, Mitch, I wanted to die.'

'Only in my arms, my love,' Mitch promised between fiery little kisses. 'Over and over again.'

Coming Next Month in Harlequin Romances!

2665 PETER'S SISTER Jeanne Allan
A battle-scarred Vietnam veteran shows up in Colorado and triggers painful memories in his buddy's sister. He reminds her of the brother she lost and the love she's never forgotten.

2666 ONCE FOR ALL TIME Betty Neels
When tragedy strikes a London nurse, support comes—not from her fiancé—but from her supervising doctor. But she finds little comfort, knowing he's already involved with another woman.

2667 DARKER FIRE Morgan Patterson
Because she so desperately needs the job, a Denver secretary lies about her marital status. But how can she disguise her feelings when her boss asks her to leave her husband and marry him instead?

2668 CHÂTEAU VILLON Emily Spenser
Her wealthy French grandfather tries to make amends for having disinherited her father. Instead, he alienates Camille and the winery's heir when he forces them to marry before love has a chance to take root.

2669 TORMENTED RHAPSODY Nicola West
The idea of returning to the tiny Scottish village of her childhood tantalizes and torments a young Englishwoman. Inevitably, she'll run into the man who once broke her heart with his indifference.

2670 CATCH A FALLING STAR Rena Young
Everyone in the music business calls her the Ice Maiden. But there's one man in Australia capable of melting her reserve—if only to sign her with his nearly bankrupt recording company.

Introducing
Harlequin Intrigue

Because romance can be quite an adventure.

Available in August wherever paperbacks are sold.

INT-3